SUGAR, SMOKE, SONG

SUGAR, SMOKE, SONG

a novel

Reema Rajbanshi

2018
Red Hen Press
WOMEN'S
PROSE
PRIZE

Red Hen Press | *Pasadena, CA*

Library of Congress Cataloging-in-Publication Data

Names: Rajbanshi, Reema, 1981– author.
Title: Sugar, smoke, song : a novel / Reema Rajbanshi.
Description: Pasadena : Red Hen Press, [2020]
Identifiers: LCCN 2019049314 (print) | LCCN 2019049315 (ebook) | ISBN
  9781597098915 (trade paperback) | ISBN 9781597098908 (ebook)
Subjects: LCSH: Young women—Fiction. | Asian American women—Fiction. |
  Experimental fiction, American.
Classification: LCC PS3618.A4335 .S84 2020 (print) | LCC PS3618.A4335
  (ebook) | DDC 813/.6—dc23
LC record available at https://lccn.loc.gov/2019049314
LC ebook record available at https://lccn.loc.gov/2019049315

The National Endowment for the Arts, the Los Angeles County Arts Commission,
the Ahmanson Foundation, the Dwight Stuart Youth Fund, the Max Factor Family
Foundation, the Pasadena Tournament of Roses Foundation, the Pasadena Arts &
Culture Commission and the City of Pasadena Cultural Affairs Division, the City
of Los Angeles Department of Cultural Affairs, the Audrey & Sydney Irmas Char-
itable Foundation, the Kinder Morgan Foundation, the Meta & George Rosenberg
Foundation, the Albert and Elaine Borchard Foundation, the Adams Family Foundation, the Riordan Foundation, Amazon Literary Partnership, and the Mara W.
Breech Foundation partially support Red Hen Press.

First Edition
Published by Red Hen Press
www.redhen.org

Acknowledgments

So many well-wishers crossed my path as this manuscript took shape over eight-plus years.

Brave writers taught me literature was serious business: Patricia Powell, Pam Houston, Lucy Corin, Riché Richardson, Chris Abani, Elmaz Abinader, and Anna Joy Springer. Thank you for believing I had something to say.

California friends became the family this book needed: Alan and Alicia Brown, Antoinette Rose Mendieta, Carolyn Menard, Michael Robinson, Moazzam Sheikh, Pranami Mazumdar, Seeta and Sambhu, Tsomo and Samten, Maché, Bascom, Chloe, and Brian. Your love and jokes saw me through the harder years.

To friends and family in New York City, Northeast India, and Brazil: thank you for sharing the lessons of your struggles and the ferocity of your art over hearty momos and drinks!

To all those who read drafts of these stories or who published them, especially the clear-sightedness of Kate Gale and her hardworking team at Red Hen Press: thank you for the essential magic of building a reading community.

And to my parents and grandparents: thank you for passing on the indelible value of literacy and how, for some of our dreams, it is never, ever too late.

Deuta (Bimal Rajbanshi),
for the gifts of faith and revision.

Contents

SUGAR, SMOKE, SONG

The Ruins

My sister's left me to the night. Its mouth of stars, this glass between them and me, this bed where I lie in half. She's left me for that half-breed sister, Assam, arms she'd thrust in mine spread for jungle, legs she'd wrapped me with run for hills. To the ruins hidden there, carved with stories wearing off with rain.

All I've got are mute stars in a black Bronx sky, and no sister to name the fiercest bits. "Scorpion, the Hunter, the Bear," she'd say, pressing her finger to the glass. "And Gemini. Twins like us. Split personalities." But no twin tonight, palm on navel, lip on shoulder, to rein me in with what else she'd seen. "Maina, the crazy on our corner tried talking to me. Took off his cap, started tap dancing. Maina, did you know mice pee when they die? I saw it in the lab. Dr. Klein had me etherize fourteen."

So I take what's left, my sister's most private thing. In a blue book shelved behind the others, Biju recorded her life in even cursive: the eggs, the clouds, the rattling number five, how well the slides of brain tissue magnified one evening. I rip her pages and spread them on the floor—I know I should be last of all to take my sister's words—but rules have never stopped me.

She's crammed the lines, scribbled the letters as if worried someone might read her. And archaeologist that I hope to be, I will decode her script. Here she kept her one true language, while all the rest was ruse, silence snaking a tomb.

Mom knocks in and too late, I shield the page, 'cause up I glance at my sister's wary eyes, hear the pause that won't prod me when there's nothing I want to confess. Only when mom shuffles out do I smooth that first yellowed page and think: my sister was good, she was smart, she was better than me.

June 18, 2003

A week since he came at me. I couldn't even tell what for. Not then, not now. All I saw was his face. Pasty white with shot, rolling eyes. The knife swirling at me like he was hacking through brush. Everyone keeps asking, How'd it feel? Fire. Like pricks of fire zipping 'cross my face. And the blood. It didn't spill like in the movies, just welled up in lines, like I had a hundred paper cuts. Down my nose, round my mouth, on my lids, my vessels sliced on both cheeks. I didn't scream either. Just froze, like I was stuck in a block of ice and here was this master artist come to carve me out. Bring me out to life.

He muttered when he walked away. I think I slid, on one of those subway columns. Our train was whizzing by. Angry, clanging, rushing east. Maina was running, too frantic to make a sound, going west for anybody. Through all those people who didn't do *nothing*. Just stood there like it was a show and everybody was supposed to be polite and watch. When she knocked on the ticket booth glass, the MTA guy raised a palm. "Honey," he said. "You see the line. Get on the back of it."

Thank God the doors opened when they did. The conductor shouted for the cops. Maina was holding me. She was trembling. "Wake up," she said. "Don't die." I wanted to tell her, It's fine. He didn't get my heart or my guts or my kidney. Just my face. I'm still alive.

But white blots were blooming all over. Mouths were opening and the sound was off. Stars bursting up-close. I could hear my breath, going so fast it was like that was what kept my heart pumping.

Biju forgot some things and lied about others. She forgot to say how the cops caught the guy, who'd loped away like a giraffe, swinging his long limbs, the knife slick and bright in his blue-veined hands. His glide was amazing, really, like some slow-motion shot in a black-and-white film, where everyone's frozen except the villain and the victim, and the only color is red, that one streak on the villain's knife, which grows smaller, and the rivulets seeping into the victim's shirt, then her sister's jeans.

'Cause there I was, kneeling on the platform, holding Biju's face between my hands, trying to stopper the blood that was dribbling like tomato juice from a broken bottle. There he went, ambling easily along the platform, veering into the crowd that parted like he was Moses or something. A Dominican man with the inflated chest of a superhero sprinted and jumped the guy, threw him down on the platform's broad yellow stripe, then pinned his scrawny arms back.

Biju lied about what she said as she lay in my lap. She didn't say she'd be fine. She was crying, her words garbled, the blood bubbling from her lips. She shut her slanted eyes, the only tribal trait I could find in the marred rises of her face, and asked, "Maina, what's happening?" I was the one who felt I'd vomit on my sister's shambles. I was the one who said, for her and for myself, "Shh, just breathe, stay awake."

Biju didn't write about the hospital, though every time the ambulance jerked, she'd turn her face to check on me. The medics had covered her with rolled washcloths to soak up the blood, but still, they set the mask unclipped, so its edges wouldn't bite her cheeks. With every breath, that mask fogged and cleared, showing her tender lizard tongue curled under her red-stained teeth.

For thirty minutes, I paced the hall alone, until nurses wheeled

Biju into the ICU. In filed our procession, Mom, Dad, and friends circling her shrouded body, pliant plastic tube forcing itself out her mouth, nervous green line on the heart monitor beeping and jumping. The women stared and the men fidgeted, while someone led Dad out through the curtains. They wouldn't let me follow, but still I could hear him, we all could. It was like nothing I'd ever heard from a man, a noise bursting out in fits, so fierce it filled our room, must've rung in the hall where he sat, an animal sound that demanded privacy and listening.

July 15, 2003

Dr. Perry fixed my face, though I haven't seen his yet, just felt his hand smoothing out my brow when they laid me down this morning. If Maina were here, she'd say, That's okay, hands tell you everything. She wouldn't talk about The Thing, his sickly arms, the veins bulging like they were gonna burst, the knife his fingers gripped.

After the attack, she'd point out hands to me on the train. "Look," she'd say. "The old man in his bowler hat, paper covering his face: a thinking man, sharp knuckles, spare fingers. Or here, the guy in his paint-splattered duds, slumped against the silvery wall: brutish hands, rough skin, but see the palms slip off the knee, soft and scarred inside like Dad's. Or there and there," the hands of men who'd look Maina up and down, wouldn't flinch when she cold-stared them back: mottled hands, lotioned fingers sliding up and down the poles.

I'd tell her, "No, I believe in faces." All those train rides, all I'd notice were eyes darting away, glancing again, dropping to the floor. Kids pinched their cheeks this way and that, even the adults stared and whispered. In the glass behind them, I'd catch my scars, red like wires mashed into my face.

But I've got no sister to tell now, gone tramping through jungle for clues to our past. "Good luck," I'd whispered our last night in bed, but I want her here, below this sky I've named, its face shielding hers and mine.

I should be grateful to have a sister so fearless, so pretty. That's how I got my surgery for free. Dr. Perry is Josh's dad; Josh is the Jewish boy who told Maina he'd do anything for her, even wipe my scars down to almost nothing. "Almost," I said to Maina my first night back, and had her finger the pink ridges. "If you look hard enough, the marks are still there." Then Maina whispered back to me: she only kept him around for my sake. When she shivered into my arms, I warmed her cheeks with mine, but wondered if her soft bedtime eyes were real, or if she always grabbed what she needed, then up and left for something better.

Biju was right about the taking. After the slashing, I couldn't seem to stop. First there was the gauze, rolls and rolls I grabbed from the drawer by her hospital bed. Then there was the stuff rich girls get easy—foundation, cocoa butter, cream—which I swiped from stores, anything she and I might need. A month later, flying into Assam, I was taking everything.

On the Mumbai plane, I rummaged through the purse of the woman sleeping next to me, saved the batteries I thought might come in handy, an address book for when I'd have to call somebody. In the terminal to Guwahati, I grabbed sandwiches from the counter, handed them to urchins wandering barefoot on the shiny airport floor. I couldn't stand to see them, so young and sullied, calling out with wants people were ignoring. By the week I trekked for those ruins, I had a practiced hand, and whatever I fancied, palace stone or temple carving, any fractured thing, I took.

Though the stone I wanted most, I couldn't move. Narasingha, mane loose, tongue out, in the middle of rubble that was Ukha's palace. Even rain, which hits this earth harder than any other, wearing the rock-carved gods off their chariots, couldn't topple that image: God come to save a boy. He was a prince, who wouldn't pray to the king, so the king decided to kill his son. The man was crazed with himself and made so by the gods, who'd promised him no death, day or night, on earth or sky, by animal or man. And yet God heard and came at dusk, a lion's head on a man's body, and lay the king on his lap and ripped him wide with his claws.

Running my hands over that cold carving was like touching the new contours of my sister's face. How was she caught on this hill, in Ukha's house? Centuries before the British and Tai-Ahom named us Assamese, a tribal king had set magic stones to guard his daughter. On top, he posted his sentinels to watch her sleep, and on bottom, lit a circle of fire so no man could touch her. Still his kingdom crumbled—only the hill survived.

When I returned to the Bronx, my sister had stopped talking. Biju would not leave the bed till noon, would not walk out onto the pulsing streets where men will not let a pretty girl go without a comment and a damaged girl pass without a laugh. She would not breathe a sound as she ate rice or watched TV or roamed the house like a phantom—what I could have been. Nothing could shake her out, not my photos of the hill people, not the Himalayan jewelry I'd haggled over, not the birthday fiesta Mom and Dad threw to warm her with friends, make life look normal, celebrate what we hoped was a new beginning.

August 30, 2003

Big party in the basement for our sweet sixteen. Sweet, I suppose, 'cause I'm alive, my face intact, scars partly gone, Maina back on Bronxwood Avenue. Though I can't help hating whatever the hell did this to me and not to her. We were alike as two people split from an egg can be until The Thing came up—slice!—life cut me and Maina in half again.

Mom says it would've happened sooner or later; Dad says we were always different, that no matter what, I'm a beautiful girl, someone will come who sees my exact beauty. Though I can't buy lines like that anymore. What I hear are people saying around the table of White Castle burgers, to Mom and Dad, *We were so sorry to learn,* or to me, *Mami, you look so much better,* or to Maina, *Wow, this one'll make the boys go mad.*

Maina hears it all and pulls me upstairs to our bedroom, where we find ourselves before the mirror. Like looking at a before and after shot, or split halves of the god-and-goddess pair, Shiva-Kali. Maina, the regal mountain god, loinclothed in animal print, and me, his blue and angry wife with her bleeding tongue. We stare at what remains the same, heart-shaped faces, Mom's buttercream coloring, her slender Aryan frame, the tribal eyes we got from Dad, his straight hair, the sideways glance we give everybody but each other.

It's Maina who turns away, who cannot face the contrast. She rummages in the drawer for a scent, telling me how she stole the bottle, how it smells like jasmine, the flower that grew thick in Assam. "The ruins," she says, "Biju, they were amazing. Man, those ruins are us, they're our history." In the mirror, my eyes eclipse, and I find in them all the things Maina describes: fish flashing silver through the river, shadows cast by bamboo fronds, embers of wood coal as they glow, then fade. My face swells in the mirror, slashed over and over like the corpses piling in the jungles of Assam, lines the British drew on hills and plains they took from the Burmese, all the ways Indians watch tribal faces but turn from them too. My fine, mutilated face looms in the mirror, and I think, I am my history, I am my history, I am my history.

After that summer, Biju and I no longer sat in the same classes, never teamed up on handball. The autumn horde pushed us down opposite aisles, Biju to bio, me to archaeology. So that late into evening, I'd compile photos of ruins in an abandoned room while Biju stood outside on the sidelines of the court. The girls huddled without her, the boys rattled the chain-link, chanting *Barface B.* My sister crossed the street, then bussed to lab where she'd wash brain tissue for hours, read the paper front to back.

Even at lunch, when boys eyeing our derrieres, which must've looked exactly the same, sat at our table, an execution light turned on. They couldn't help it—they'd look and speak to me. They wouldn't give my sister another glance, pretend to be polite, remember there was a body identical to mine sitting between us. I tried once to rise, but Biju held my elbow down. "I don't blame them and I don't blame you."

So I dated one and another and another. I wrote a list of penances I was paying:

Thanksgiving: Jacob Stein, lanky, Jewish, sixteen. Pedantic, cocky, snorted when he laughed. Never topped three minutes.

Christmas: Drake Lloyd, articulate, black, eighteen. Smart, slacker, sexy. Best phone technique around. Bedside manner lousy.

February: Ravi Gupta, hairy Gujrati monkey, eighteen. Cheated three times. Smallest dick in high school history.

March: Ray Soto, slender, Puerto Rican, sixteen. Gentle, sweet, boring.

April: Tommy Storelli, Riverdale boy, *Godfather* speak, seventeen. Rich, crazy, druggie.

On and on, in dark cramped rooms, the stalls of public baths, the benches of parks, and yet the boys, their sweat, their stupid fumbling ways were all the same. As they nuzzled their noses in my neck or wound down my torso with their lips, they'd murmur, "Man, you're fine." It was then, no matter where I lay, whatever ceiling or sky I saw, I would hate them, know that whatever it was they liked, they couldn't really *see* me. Always in the night, I would ask, "Do you think my sister's pretty?" The dumb ones yawned, "Nah, you guys look so different, we would never mix you up." The sly ones answered, "Sure, yeah, your sister's sweet."

Biju'd lie in bed till I crept back, and not once asked where I'd been, what I'd done. Still, I told her, naming this one's stinky moves, that one's stinky breath. Still, she'd never speak, just tap her finger on my navel—until the sun flowered the dogwoods on the parkway and merengue filled the warm subway cars. Then Biju opened the window and rolled over to ask, "How do you get a guy? How do you please him?" I wanted to say, *Why, give them what they want— something untroubled by time, something easy—when none of that is real?* But I kissed my sister instead and whispered what I knew, and that's how Biju landed Nikhil Reddy.

May 1, 2004

Maina's ways were weird on me.

I sputtered fast to Nikhil about the school dance but, in the discoed-out cafeteria, couldn't look him in the eye. I tried anyways to rub my back against him, letting my hair fall on half my face. Would you believe what he said? "I can't see you", and turned me round, brushed my hair behind my ears.

I took him to the Coney Island beach, where he dared me to strip into the water. I shivered as I bared myself—but waded in. And he followed, glasses and shorts still on, mouth open, little belly quivering. On the train platform, rubbing the feeling back into my toes, he said, "You're braver than I thought." I pulled my feet away and said, "Everyone's looking." And what did he do but hold my hand, the whole subway ride, till we reached Morris Park. Even then, past the stop signs, into the house, where the sun slanted through my bedroom blinds, he wouldn't let go. Just took his glasses off and toasted my palms against the bed.

It was only when Nikhil took me to the Met that I got to look. Not at the mummies in their fake pyramids, but at his face: copper orb on my lap, while over me, glass roof. The sun sliced onto his veined lids, his crooked nose, though to the guard twirling his stick up, we were just brown kids. "Keep moving," he said, but I steeled my thighs until the guard poked them and sent us scurrying to the train. I was the one to press Nikhil's hand between mine, all the way to Morris Park where, I'd forgotten, Maina would come meet us. She narrowed her black eyes into knives at our clasp, and said no wazzup, no nothing. Only at night, Nikhil gone, did my sister roll her back to me and say, "I guess my tactics worked."

Biju's guy was unreal: a chubby Mr. Smiley-Face, soft voice and soft ways, devoted to a girl no other guy seemed to want. I watched him at family dinners, the way he grinned into her face, even fingered once the line running down her jaw. And how she bloomed, a sudden rose, hands rushing up to hold her petaled cheeks together. But his hands, pristine like they'd been soaking in rose water, gave away nothing, nor did his eyes, hidden by dark round discs.

What else could the motherfucker want, but to bang my sister, then leave her? And if he stuck around, what sort of fetish freak was he? When I cornered him by the lockers, asked him what his intentions were, he laughed, said not even my parents had asked him that! But the slick operator never took her to restaurants and clubs where they could be seen. It was always nestle by our living room TV, moon over our deck at the fig tree, rustle about in the bedroom that was also mine.

They had locked me out. Worse, Biju was letting him do something with her I couldn't do anything about. The gasping, the tiny cries, a stabbing I couldn't see—a train whirred through my ears.

Not again.

I ran out to the streets, where cars slowed to catcall me, where shopmen turned to rate my tits, my ass, where a million girls-mommies-grannies marched on by. I ran right at the columns of the subway track, and pressed my back against the quivering steel leg.

This was where.

Even with my eyes shut, I saw that boy's manicured hands, groping my sister's pieces, his blank face grunting over her shattered one. Then I knew, as terrible as it would look, what I had to do. For her, for us. Later, I'd tell her, we were twins, we were each other's trustees, only we knew and loved each other's ruins. No matter what, no matter who, we had to stick together through everything.

She tried to steal him from me. No other way to put it. I came home from lab, where half the mice had died, falling slack in their own pool of urine. When I pushed open the door to those odd slidings and snaps, I found them rattling my shelf of notes. His hand under the crease of her behind, her calf flexed up, nails curling about his chin. Even here, I can't name their expressions, just how quickly their faces parted.

His glasses were on, still, as he was doing my sister—what did he need to see?—and I saw my mouth reflected there. Cracked wide like a mask, to the darkness within. What a village boy must've seen when he asked God to open his—*are you really who you say you are*—and Krishna had revealed the whole world swirling inside.

Well, there was my world till now, staring at me with the eyes of a frightened fawn, my figure centered in both orbs. She drew her blouse together, stretched her hand to me, and said fast, "Biju, there was a reason for this. Let me explain." But I heard the whirr of trains, my sister's feet running far, from me to them. So that when she stepped to touch me, I stepped behind that door, breath caught at last. I asked it loud then, for us both, "How could you do this to me?"

Yes, that's how it looked, but if Biju had stayed in our room, if she hadn't run east to those ruins I'd left for her, I would've explained. A boy who'd do her in for nothing more or less than her own sister wasn't worth our time. 'Cause no matter what, I'd always returned, from all those boys and buildings, to this room and bed. I'd always come collect her. I needed her to remember this was all.

So I write my ending to her book.

Nothing else, sister, matters. One more boy, another hour of fun—those moments die. What stands is the structure where those moments were, even if it's in pieces. The house the tribal king built for his daughter, a palace of love, a palace of stone, every rock marked with what we run toward: the feasting, the fighting, the vengeful gods.

I lie in our bed tonight, lit by what's left to us both, stars smashed against glass. And I touch my finger to the sky that must arc over my sister too, wherever she's stowed, among the hills and ruins and their quiet, haunting voices.

BX Blues:
A Dance Manual
for Heartbreak

PROLOGUE

This is a story, a dance, a ride in several parts. This is a story of how God saved the world, ten times in ten forms, when times got tough. This is a story of time. What the old books called Yugas, each epoch less and less graced by truth. What the regulars call train stops, each place closer or further from home. This is a manual for how to re-piece heartbreak, how to dance through wrongs, how to last a ride freighted with memory.

INTRODUCTORY DANCE ACT

First, you must clear the stage and cast a back screen.

You, Biju, are the dokhavatar, who gestures each of the ten avatars to the stage. You, Maina, are God, who leaps into each avatar, then rests your hands into a flute by your face.

You, Biju, wear white lined with gold, a Nehru cap over your bun, and only pearls on your ears. You, Maina, wear gold silk and a blue velvet cape. A peacock feather in your loose hair and bright rings on every finger.

You, Biju and Maina, must move your hands at every chorus interval like a blooming lotus, a spinning world. You must slide your

feet in a four-step slowly: keeping heel circles small, spinning on the
last four-step, pressing that back-cross toe firmly.

STOP 1

Ali Baba: the train doors part. You slide to the corner seat, close
your eyes to the light, to faces you'll always see and never know—
Kosovar mothers with deep brows, Old World kerchiefs, black men
with arms crossed, Timberlands splayed, all the riders bent over
milk and bread and candles, pursed mouths guarding their own
train stories.

Things are like this: you and Biju, who once roamed the city in
matching brown puffy coats, are lucky if you speak once a year. You
train up, the last to know of her engagement, at a dinner where
she gifted you *pearls*, she laughed, *she didn't need*. Why shouldn't
you gift her the mannequin you've been piecing from city trash, a
mosaic that might rise and wave, *what can I sing, bhonti, to bring*
you back?

Can I sing a bihu, those Oxomiya blues we danced before we could
walk? Ma swathed us in gold mekhlas and we watched each other
for every pentatonic stop. Can I sing a borgeet, those devotionals
we clapped to every full moon? The four of us washed and seated,
heads bowed as Baba rubbed brass taals, singing for salvation, for
forgiveness. Can I sing the American blues you loved, fluttery notes
of Si Sé, Alicia, Mariah lifting over rain-splattered streets while you
spread-eagled on your bed, hopeful in the dark?

The train heaves on to stop two—you can barely carry a note—
and real people curl up around you like morning glories.

MATSYA

Some of you have Noah who built the ark, some of you have King
Manu who built a boat. In that story, God himself becomes a fish
to anchor the boat, to keep its two- and four-feathered-limbed sail-
ors and the tsunamied world from dissolving. It was still the Age

of One Hundred Percent Truth, but a demon had stolen the Vedas, and without this book (lo! the power of stories!), the Age would end without the world being made anew.

So God swam deep into the ocean where the demon had buried the book, and bellied it up for readers to come. Then God swam, a tiny silver thing, into Manu's hands, and begged him to save his life. King Manu's compassion cradled the fish into a bowl, then a tank, then a river, then an ocean, as the little nickelback plumped into a silver-shackled-barrucada of a thousand whales, who warned Manu of the coming flood in seven days.

When it was all over, God lay flopping, silvery small on the sand, gills heaving, as if saving the world had been deadlier than making it.

DANCE ACT I

Stage glows silver and blue, as if you were in an ocean. Cast swirls of blues and grays across the screen, to mimic currents.

You, Biju, and you, Maina, must creep in slow unison, palms atop each other, thumbs circling like fins. You must slide in the four-step time: right heel kick front, left toe back-cross, right heel in place step, alternating right-left, till you reach the front of the stage.

Kneel, then slowly rise. With palms shooting up, thumbs circling fast, to indicate God swimming fast, for all our dear lives.

STOP 2

Biju, do you remember the afternoon I lost you?

It rained the way it does today—slanted torrents erasing everything till the clouds breathed five, four, three . . . and I shielded your fuzzy sleeping head on my shoulder. Boys with their puffy coats and unfettered manes hung by the closest pole, commenting on your milky rose, your delicate wrists. "I'd marry her for her cheeks," they conferred.

I shook you—our stop—but when I dashed out the doors, you

rose frantic-eyed. The train slipped off—your palms pressed to the glass—I laughed and waited till you rode back.

Your cards, when you ran onto the platform and showed me, had disintegrated into blue scraps. I could only make out two equations—$E=mc^2$ and $F=ma$. "Energy and force," you said woefully, "are the only things that made it."

Look how, Biju, a decade later, I've discovered a third: $E + F = L$, a hidden love, brash and raw and too blue to bury. How we are all the wild childs of the city, train-riding some afternoons, crush-jumping in the dark, with our frank glances, our sweet rumps, springs when merengue jiggles on car after car of tank tops and shorts, summers when we have to bust a hydrant to cool the roads down, all the goosebumpy nights we whisper. *Yo mami, hi ma, hey bhonti, ki khobor Biju, come home, okay?*

KURMA

God becomes a tortoise in the very first race. The gods and demons had made a truce—all to churn up the nectar of immortality from the ocean of milk—but the mountain they'd turned into a churning staff began to sink. So God morphed his back into a dappled bowl, his ancient face you can't help but love rolling its eyes like, *I can't believe I have to save these kids from themselves.* The gods and demons went back to pulling each end of a snake, the mountain re-birthing the foaming pot of nectar, so that each side rushed at a taste of *Forever.*

Here's the part they never tell you: God had to shapeshift again, into the jewel-eyed, honey-pussied Mohini to lure the demons away from the other Nectar, and into Shiva the Destroyer, who had to drink up the poison that also poured forth. His was the first throat to turn blue. Even then, God couldn't stop one demon from swallowing immortality, and though he cut the demon's head, the head lives, every now and then swallowing the sun.

Dance Act II

Shadowbox power players across the back screen. Let rise a mountain, let sink the mountain, a snake's wriggle darkening the screen, the stage, the audience.

At such a moment, you, Biju and Maina, stay together, from the back wing to center stage to front wing, in that simple four-step. Your hands too are basic, palms still overlapping but thumbs hidden. Swimming, sliding as shelled creatures do. But once at the front, you must split-shift, as God does.

Biju, you face front-right and become Mohini the Temptress, cocking your hip, resting mudra-ed hand to your ample bum, cupping your back head with an arched, suggestive arm to distract the bad boys. Maina, you face front-right and become blue-throated Shiva, kneeling and cupping your palms to catch the poison, tipping back your face to the eclipsing moon to drink in death, to save immortality for the good kids before the lights go out.

Stop 3

Don't say names, or smell Old Spice mixed with sweat, or watch that brassy face sit before you, conjuring him up. The city's *haunted* by jawlines that slope like his, by crisp white shirts unbuttoned at the top, by hands dangling from overhead holds with the same gibbon grace. Today's twin smiles at you, above his head, the ticker line flashes—12:20—and you think, déjà vu means riding with ghosts.

The afternoon your long-gone man sat by you, he said, "It's warmer over here."

"A window's open," you said, measuring the bangs that slanted his brow.

Van Gogh's wheat is what you saw, not his toothpaste smile that meant untried youth, his rum-and-coke breath that meant bachelor ways. Art was the problem. You had to find muscle under the skin, see if yes, those anatomy lessons were right. Lie down and he'll bend his spine. Arch your neck and he'll tilt his skull. Grip his shoulder and he'll hold your waist, playing his fingerbones over all the tones of you.

Art was shit. In a painting, the subject never moved, but a human being could walk in and out the frame of your days. Art never told you: one evening, while drinking soup, he'd say, "I'm tired. This isn't working. Let's be friends." Truth is: only art stays.

You painted your long-gone's face on a pale, blue tile and cemented it heart-smack at the center-right of your mosaic.

Baraha

This might be the least flattering avatar of all: God the wild, white boar. Oh, he was beautiful even then, but the plot twist begs the question, does God save some at the expense of others, all for Himself?

He'd turned into a long-tusked boar with shiny, white spindles when Hiranyaksha, an immortal human, gathered the ball of earth under his bicep crook and dove to the bottom of the unbreathable sea. The arrogant kid was looking to pick a fight with Vishnu, God's Preserver form, who was the only one stronger than him. So God the boar wrestled with the kid for a thousand years and, after slicing the kid's head with his disc, lifted the Earth like a dark pearl on his glistening tusks.

Thing was, Hiranyaksha had only ever become human because he had once been God's godly bodyguard and, on duty, had blocked four other gods from bothering his master's sleep. Those gods had cursed Hiranyaksha to human life but promised, when an apologetic Vishnu awoke, Hiranyaksha would be relieved when Hiranyaksha met his death at God's hands.

You tell me: what kind of reward is death for a duty done? How come Hiranyaksha never was reborn when he lost his only home? How come, for us to live, Hiranyaksha had to die?

Dance Act III

Cast against a roiling screen of blue-and-black waves, clangs of thun-

der and steel, bellows of enraged bulls. Girls, charge in fast on your three-step, hands in a cowabunga sign that means tusks, by your cheeks. At the front center, close to each other, jump onto your right knee, then rise in a wave sway, as if lifting the world on your hand-tusks. Keeping your right hand up by your right cheek, grab with your left hand your string of dark costume pearls. Tug them loose, glare with squinted eyes and pouted mouth at the audience, while a hundred earths scatter and lose their way.

STOP 4

Halfway there now. Parking lot: Julian and Abe pass a blunt, watch the girls wafting by. C-town: Mr. Chakraborty walks to his Toyota, weightlifting a bag of soda, a bag of carp. Flower show: Mr. Lee jabs lilies into a base, while Maribel flicks through roses for her quinceañera. Train tracks: Felicia and Eve teach Patrick double Dutch, chanting, sticking gum on the ramp.

Strangers step off these streets and, for several minutes, ride with you, blank faces that'll disappear into night, that mean *home* when you're far enough away. Church ladies dozing in bright hats; brothers brushing their iPod screens; Bangladeshis clutching kids like precious cargo. You wanted them reflected in your gift, so you painted that mannequin taupe brown, laid on it a straight, black wig, and cemented your map, square by square, on it. Now, you've got one tile missing, right on the face, and nothing left to say.

You too stared wordlessly, *bhonti*, from the mud one afternoon.

You'd run backward from the Assamese barbeque, calling "Maina, come faster," so that you'd be sure I was following you to the sandbox of American kids. *Plop!* your beaming moon face creased into fault lines of terror—back you fell into a mudhole.

"How did this happen?" You wept as you rose, arms like broken wings. "Ma will be so mad." You pointed to the leopard print jumper she'd stitched for us.

Back at the barbeque pit, where chuckling men sipped *saa* and pointed, Ma slapped your tush. Yanked the comb through your muddy curls. Tugged on a younger kid's green shorts and shirt. You sobbed, not wanting to be a brown boy. "That's what you get," Ma said, "for going too far."

Even now, when your trussed-up self won't glance this way, I cannot laugh.

BAMUNA

God becomes a dwarf to reclaim the three worlds from an over-powerful king. You wouldn't think revolutions work this way, would you, but in the Age of the Truth, they did. So he walked up, under his monk's umbrella, to the throne circled by guards, vixens, leashed tigers. And because it was the day of alms-giving, Bali the king agreed to give whatever Bamuna's little heart desired. *Three plots of land*, Bamuna said quietly, *as large as my footsteps.* Bali laughed—austerity had clearly driven the midget mad—and said, against his counselor's whispers, *so be it.*

And the dwarf grew—as large as the king—and grew—as large as the banyan—and grew—as large as the kingdom—and grew—till his first step covered the whole earth—*boom*—till his second step covered the heavens—*whoosh*—till, with his third and last step, he gently toe-pressed the ant-like king all the way down to hell.

DANCE ACT IV

Stage glows gold but, as Bamuna grows and steps one-two-three, glows red. Show an arrogant man seated on the back screen.

Walk in on your knees, taking tiny steps, gripping an imaginary handle with the left hand, forming an umbrella cover with the right hand. Standing head-bent before the audience, sweep your arms in a circle and rise, first your right leg, then your left leg. Fisting your hips, lunge forth with power: right-one! Left-two! But on the third step, lift your right leg with the toes pointed straight down, and slowly drop

your leg till the big toe touches the stage. Keep your head up, for this
finale moment is an act of mercy.

STOP 5

The site of crime, the point of brilliance. You found gold carnage on
the pavement, necklaces and bracelets and rings leading like Doro-
thy's road around the block. Fake stuff, you figured, so you grabbed
what you could from looters, and melted enough for one gold arm.
Your mannequin's moneymaker, holding a trowel the way you do
when you're cementing one gold tile, then another.

The thing about gold tiling is, each tile shines a different spot of
light, so the arm ripples to muscle when you walk around. The Byz-
antines did this, used walls of gold to background dark-eyed men,
to make them come alive. They knew the luster of yellow, why art
should say decadent things even when it was holy.

Fifteen centuries between those walls and you, but right away
those images are your own: solemn Jewish faces, formal stances of
Russian and Indian immigrants, the gold and the darkness that are
Bronx summer nights. The dead speak, though apparently not everyone listens.

A night like this, you found a loose train label, the number two
in a big green circle. You pasted it on your mannequin's chest, for
half the beats lost underground. The next night, you found a photo,
you and your parents at a street fair, days before they crashed. Another two goes up beside the first. Suddenly, you can't stop, scaveng-
ing the city for what it's done. A silver scrap from the car wreck off
the Major Deegan; fish scales from the Fulton Market walk; green
streamers from the St. Patty's Day parade.

You paste them all, square by square, a city map exploding on
your junkheap find.

NARAXINGHA

The only other avatar who could give Naraxingha a run for his money is Kalki, the avatar yet to come, brandishing a thunder sword and riding on a white horse, in the Kalya Yuga or Dark Age to save the people from themselves. Kalki, who might as well come now.

But what we've got is Naraxingha, who outwitted power that looks as maniacal as it does now, a Nietzschean king who thought he could out-God God. He commanded the people to worship him alone and when his son, a pure-hearted thing, refused, the king prepared to kill his own blood. And because the gods/powers-that-be had blessed this king with impunity—he couldn't be killed by man or animal, day or night, on land or sea—God came at dusk, spanked that king on his human lap, and tore him open with his lion claws.

And the little brown boy, who had been put in the juvie of his age, sprang out. Vindicated, mischievous, free.

DANCE ACT V

The stage glows red. Cast a fire on the back screen.

Slide in sweeping arcs of the legs to the center. Pounce into wide stance, as if in a Maori haka. Raise your arms like a body shield, fingers curved into claws. Your face must go into Kali-Durga-all-the-warrior-goddesses-ever mode: eyes wide, nostrils flaring, tongue out. Breathe fire.

As you and Biju stand one-legged, do not totter, do not laugh. The audience might. This is one gesture of fear. They may even fall asleep. This is another.

STOP 6

A pink-shirted, moth-lashed Puerto Rican man lay his head by your lap once while you pretended to read. "Hola guapa," he said. "What big eyes you have, what a straight nose, such a pretty little pout." Great, you thought—the words blurring before you—Little Indian Riding Hood and the Big Puerto Rican Wolf. *Please dear gods, let him get off or let me.*

The last car was no better, with a roly-poly black man sitting alone, pushing up his taped glasses. Rub-a-dub went his hand over his gray pants, his mouth open as if he couldn't breathe. Neither could you, your heart zooming with the tracks till the doors jerked wide.

You ran past the cops, their puggish Irish faces, their useless swagger round the token booth. "Whatcha readin', sweetheart?" the blonde one said. You lifted up your book, *Dada in New York*, and walked the steps backward, away from the city's most dangerous men.

"Smart *and* pretty," the broad-shouldered one said. You slid like a criminal for the exit. "Cat got your tongue?" the blond one said. "No habla inglés?"

Oh, you speak Englishes.

You speak Subway Ride: East Tremont, meaning Montefiore, the hospital where your father's wilted like a loose balloon. Not like your mother, who lay gutted in the car, the ramp pinning her to the chair.

You speak Paramedic: *your mother died on impact, your father's suffered multiple fractures and laceration of the coronary artery.*

You speak Statistics: *while the odds aren't high that your father will pull through, there's a chance, and we'll do our best to grab it.*

You speak Blog: *Mom, 9:36 a.m. Dad, 1:43 p.m. It doesn't feel real, doesn't seem fair, but it's official. I'm on my own. Another city waif.*

PARAXURAMA

Paraxurama was the original lumberjack, the son of a sage who'd been gifted an axe by Shiva, the Trinity's god of Destruction. Imagine this: also bearded but wearing only animal skins, holy beads, and that scintillating, bloody blade. Imagine this: his father and mother cry out that the simple things they've generously shared have been stolen by kings, after the people weep that their lives, their dignity are being looted by rich warriors—so Paraxurama rumbles out the hut with that blade.

He rampages the subcontinent, hewing down the greedy kings, the guilty Kshatriyas with that Blade of Cold Mercy. Like they, not his parents or the people, are so much grass. And when his rage has consumed the one percent, he walks to the pinprick ribbons of the Brahmaputra, strips to his musty skin, washes each side of his blade a hundred times, then crouches like a child and weeps.

DANCE ACT VI

Stage glows orange-and-fire, as if this were hell. Silhouettes of charging horses, of warriors clanging swords, sweep the screen.

Both of you, Biju and Maina, get to be horse and rider and God. You get to bend your arms into an L—left palm under right elbow— and chop that axe. Right arm back—drop left. Right arm back—drop right. Chop with every four-step, charging forward through the hot air of greed to the cool, watching people. At the front of the stage, you turn to mirror each other, spinning on your left foot.

Lift that right knee, raise back that axe, and shake your mane, widen your eyes. Crash down that foot, smash down that axe, till your forearms cross, bruising your twin's stiff hand, red to blue.

STOP 7

On to stop seven now, the homestretch before the home parkway. You step between the cars yourself and watch your life unfurl before you: the PS 87 playground where you first chased boys . . . the 99 cent store where you bought your underwear . . . the halal grocery where you rented your Bollywood fix.

Breakneck—it hurtles away—dark cubes shrinking behind you.

You rush on to the one green stretch of your life, the Bronx Zoo, where on fee-free Wednesdays you studied another kind of wild. Bony cheetahs sprinted like Park Avenue divas chasing a cab. An alpha bear splashed among his fur-lined ladies like some shoulder-wiggling rapper. Groundhogs, like all the immigrants you've ever known, peeped in and out of tunneled dens for any shadow that might swoop down and eat them.

Except the groundhogs you grew up with are gone. Your parents sleep with the fishes, the house they plastered sold to Chinese brothers whose Hummer bumper sticker reads, *Free Tibet*. Mr. Gianni, the painter neighbor, vanished, his body smelled rotting by the cops, under a carpet of newspaper that detailed every life but his. The kids you learned the alphabet and algebra with—Nathan Bello, Clarice Williams, Leila Lopez—are laughing, baby-raising, hustling on some Bronx block.

Who between us, Biju, has strayed furthest from the fold? Whoring for art, who has worn pearls bought by those spared life's saltwater, had caviar with veal-eaters who pleasure themselves like swine? Who has dared to be God, turning herself into the token posh folk use when they want a purgatory tour of the Bronx? Which of us, Biju, will call this free trade and which will ask *how* if this was our life, our body, our line?

RAMA

They say Rama was the perfect husband, friend, king. They say power politics cast him from Ayodhya, his kingdom by birth, into the jungle, where he lived for fourteen years as an ascetic. They say it was a darkening time—Treta Yuga, when the world was only three-fourths truthful—when another king, Ravana of Lanka, would steal his wife, Sita. This is how the saga of the Ramayana with its demons and gods and their spinning discs and magic came to be: the subcontinental war over Helen of the East.

Except Sita and Ravana never slept together—something Dravidian Pride points out—and of course, Rama won. Only with the help of monkey-men and Hanuman (my favorite, he of the endless jokes, he who did not know his own strength till push came to shove) and his true-blue bro, Lakshman, Rama killed Ravana, freed

Sita, and returned to Ayodhya where the people lamp-lit the kingdom in the first Diwali.

But I'd add, Rama made Sita take a purity test. He didn't believe
she, who'd been abducted by a strange man to another country,
could be blameless. He *shamed* her, she who'd had his twin boys
by then, who'd been careful all along. So once she proved herself to
his suspicious ass, she pulled a Medea and asked the earth to swallow her and her children whole. The earth, remembering all things,
opened her bosom and took the outcasts in.

DANCE ACT VII

*Stage glows green, to indicate you have entered a forest. Cast the re-
peated silhouettes of birds and deer scattering across the screen. You
are Rama the exile, Rama the hunter, Rama who has lost everything,
including his queen.*

*So you must patter up fast—no easy walk here—to the front-right
of the stage, and place your right hand to your forehead, to indicate
you are looking. Place your left hand to your ear to indicate you are
listening. Shimmy your neck. Then patter back diagonally to your
starting point. Bend to one knee, directly facing the audience. Stretch
out your left hand as if you were gripping a bow. Reach back to your
right shoulder with your right hand, as if drawing an arrow from a
quiver. Set your arrow for one beat. Draw your arrow back for three,
arms taut. Let the arrow fly, opening your hands to sudden starfish,
lifting your chin to the undoubted victory of good.*

STOP 8

Sudden halt, when you first fell in love, with a stranger ten years
older than your sixteen.

The city's like that: seducing you in the seconds it takes to walk
from that subway car to this one. A stroll, really, the way he eased
into the rattling dark between cars, watching the city pass him by. A
slump, into the seat across you, thumbing through the ghetto mur-

ders and penthouse divorces of the Daily News, biceps shivering like tawny faces. Spelled right over the right orb, in green curling script that read like Assamese, was a Bengali woman's name. Petite, sweet: Meena.

The next thirty minutes, you imagined her drawing those strange lines for him before he etched them on himself, them walking, skinny arm in sturdy arm, to the neighborhood parlor, themselves the exhibit, his wearing that wifebeater to display her claim to the world.

"You an artist?" he asked, nodding at your open book. *Indian Art From the Mughals On.*

With one finger, he paused your turning, and traced the dome of the Taj Mahal. "You know a couple's buried there? The world's greatest love souvenir is a tomb."

You *didn't* know that, or know what to say, so you read aloud, "Legend has it the emperor cut off the architect's hands. The masterpiece couldn't be repeated."

"Says a lot about power," the stranger said. "Be careful no one does that to you."

"Yeah, right," you said, and watched that arm swing into night, some Indian woman's name inscribed on it.

The city's like that: in one night, you fall for someone else's man, you admire a dead woman's shrine, you memorize all the ways love makes art around you. *Ay que linda,* you used to hear folks say about things you never saw until now.

Krishna

Krishna was loverboy-playaman-magician number one. First, there was the trick of his birth: he avoided getting killed by a king who'd locked his mother, the king's own sister, in jail. (The gods had known and told the king that his nephew would one day kill and conquer him.)

In the village where he'd been whisked away to, he played so

many tricks on the people for the people—saving them from demons even as he stole everyone's backyard cream—that he came to
be called the child of *Leela*, a magic that exceeds words.

As a young man so dark and beautiful, he is always painted blue,
playing the flute. A peacock's feather in his long hair, he stole every
milkmaid's skirt and heart. You see why anyone grown up praying
to him would have a playa pattern? Why the real saving isn't how
he did kill the king and free his mother, or abduct Rukmini an Assamese princess but not Radha his married love, or counsel Arjuna
through war against his own brothers in *The Mahabharata*? These
were heroics less than the *leela* of love, when he set up mirrors at
midnight in the village fields, so that he might be everywhere at once,
so that every milkmaid would think she was his, but all the while, he
was with RadhaRadhaRadha, the beloved he abandoned but whom
the people remember for the people as his greatest love of all.

Dance Act VIII

Stage shimmers red and blue, as if this were the gasping whirlpool of a
heart. But rising along the back screen are silhouettes of trees, women,
and those terribly vain, cruel, mesmerizing peacocks.

You, Biju, are the heartbreaker god, with his flowering hands, his
one leg suggestively crossed over his delicate ankle, that single blue-
and-green eye of a feather locked in his hair.

You, Maina, are Radha, dervishing about him, head cast up in
ecstasy, pausing now and then by his side to clasp your palms to your
heart, to blossom them in a whorl into a flute by your lips. The song
you cannot help singing, you poor, wild, un/lucky thing.

Stop 9

1:00 a.m. and fifteen hours till the wedding. Till you find a face for
your mannequin.

You and Biju, trained to scout for knives and kisses in a three-
mile radius, know: faces are stories, petals hiding their seeds, the

masks we wear that we become. But your face, Maina, neither east nor west, neither street nor fine, leads where?

Once upon a time, Biju would've known, but roots hacked, you're half a tree. When you tramp up icy subway steps without her skipping gait, you're half a leg. When you skate over black-iced pavement with snow mounds you'd traversed hands-held, you're half an arm. When you run your numb fingers over bare brick and hedges, their sparkly Braille edges read *there is no good gift anymore.*

Still, you nurse your four-limbed doll in this penultimate moment. You think of slapping a glass oval on the face, something like: *dear viewer, see thyself in me.* Then you think, your patrons may be unknowing, but they're not stupid. You think of filigreeing glass in the space between the tiles, but your patrons are paying to see the work done on you, not them.

You cradle your mannequin alone in the emptied-out car, your hands throbbing as if you've got no choice but to find someone to pass on the brush, let another you finish your baby's face, sign the cheekbones in broad-tipped black marker, *I was here.*

BUDDHA

They say Buddha was a tubby peacemaker, sitting free of suffering under a wide-armed Bodhi tree. Out here, far from the tree, they forget: he was a prince with no need whatsoever to look out the window, much less see the princeless begging there. Yet he looked, he saw, he left.

After wandering and wisening up at thirty-five years, he founded a new fucking religion, but the real catch was this. Not the freedom from suffering stuff but, one of the roots of it, freedom from that dirtiest of words: caste.

'Cause when Buddha closed his eyes, he began to see the whole lotus-mud thing was true. You couldn't have those living at the top without feeding off the bottom, and the bottom was really the source of all that is, untouchable though it might seem. Fragrant, full-petaled, an endless fire like the sun's.

DANCE ACT IX

Cast the trembling carcass shadow of a banyan across the stage, the walls, even the audience.

You, Biju and Maina, must saunter in like royalty—robed in silk and costume jewelry—but halfway to the stage, you must face each other. As if enacting two mirrors, remove your pink and gold studs and pearls, then your silk robes, till you are wearing only your cotton kurtas.

In slow, sweeping three-steps together, heel-step-cross to the stage front. Half-squat and open your palms as if reading a book. Leave one palm leaf up to receive. Lift one hand in the pointer-to-thumb mudra to the heart to give.

STOP 10

Open sesame: train doors part. A newborn day, and the dividers lining the platform are signed. Tags and tags of *name*-loves-*name*, crack-is-wack-*name*, stay-in-school-*name*, *name*-was-here. They've signed the station, they've claimed the street, they've written *we are the BX, remember this.*

Climb the green stairs and sing that Oxomiya spiritual your grandma sang: *gase gase pate dheele / phulo re xorai / he ramoram / phulo re xorai / phulo re xorai.* Round the curve of quiet houses and sing to the willows hunched over the buckled intersection: *gase gase pate dheele / tree by tree you pick.* Sing to the sunflowers someone has planted, by whim, in the rectangle across their fenced front: *phulo re xorai he ramoram / blooms to adorn this xorai, Lord.* Sing across the dank subway pass, where the pigeons nest, warble, and die: *phulo re xorai / a xorai of blooms.* Sing to the concrete squares between the bodega and the synagogue, between childhood and survivalhood, to the faces you will always see and never know: *phu-lo re xorai / a xorai of blooms.*

You will rub a washcloth down your mannequin's arm of gold. You will let others write themselves on its spare earthen face. You will invite all your ghosts to circle your body displayed. Home? Not yet, Ma, but you've pressed your talon to the station wall for some other city kid to read: *my heart got danced out here.*

Ode on an Asian Dog

PLANETS

Walt's eyes were luminous planets behind his glasses. They shone
as he walked Jumi to dance rehearsals, carrying her saris and bells.
They swirled as he drove her to shops where he bought the jeans and
thongs that made him whistle. They glistened as he laid her bare on
Martha Stewart blankets in sandy coves. When his teeth clenched
those enormous nipples he said were made for breastfeeding, we
cities hummed like church organs.

"Come home with me," he said that August, so she wore her red
silk dress. Not knowing his town would shimmer up golf courses
and country clubs. That his Chinese mother would dash out a split-
level Victorian like paparazzi. Jumi emerging from the car! Jumi
hunched in the living room! Jumi sidling out the bathroom! Jumi
drooling in her sleep! Our dazed subject ran into the side garden of
nodding sunflowers, poofy hydrangeas.

There Walt's father pressed a finger to his lips *shh* and re-
arranged ceramic gnomes. He was relieved, he whispered, to
meet a humble girl, asked why she looked Thai, said he'd forgotten his Hindi. Jumi settled on a vinca bed and began the
well-worn lecture: "We're Indo-Burmese. We have indigenous

traits. Assam was the last part the British added to the Raj." Mr. Singh gave the well-worn response: Disney bug eyes, mid-air freeze. Later at the kitchen counter, he rambled on about growing up with Andaman tribals. "A people," he shook a forkful of pork, "nearly extinct." Walt laughed and thumped his chest to "Witch Doctor," as if he were one himself.

I Am Ready

Who knew they'd meet at the Harvard Welcome Table? That she'd wave to him over the spoilt milk and he'd point to his nametag and grin. "I'm half 'n half, Indian-Chinese." That he'd walk her to Au Bon Pain for fresh squeezed orange juice and she'd freeze. "I don't got money to pay you back." He'd stroll off to The Yard, hands in pockets. "I'm sure I'll be seeing you around."

Three summers later, she ran after him. Walter Singh: safe enough to lose your virginity to, staid enough to dump scot-free. She invited him to troll Manhattan readings, skinny-dip on Orchard Beach, trail her at the Puerto Rican Day parade. He stuttered questions to authors, flung sand at her till she barked *quit it*, blinked at salseras through *Harry Potter* glasses.

When she visited his Chinatown digs, he played India Arie. "Ready for Love" wafted through his boat-strewn room. Planets pooling, pooling. She straddled his lap, nibbled his ear, and begged, "Give it to me, give it to me."

"Jumi," he whispered into her black tangles, "please don't get bored with me."

Homies Forever

Mira, her Puerto Rican roomie would say. *I saw the signs.* Vero heard how Walt and three friends had trudged from the Bronx Zoo to Jumi's house with that deer-in-the-headlights look. (*Black people! Single moms! FOBs!*) Her father met them on the cherry-lined street, wearing his *Harvard Dad* T-shirt and best dentures. He waved them though the two-story brick to its warm kitchen, where he'd fried *pakora* and *masor koni*, brewed Darjeeling with cinammon. Walt & Co. sidled about corners as if walls might crash down, headlines flashing across their faces: *Harvard kids buried in Bronx apocalypse.* Mr. Saikia recited his favorite *Tales from the Crypt*: who got robbed at gunpoint, who got shoved onto the tracks, who got raped in the park. Jumi, trying not to giggle, snorted tea in and out her nose.

Months later, Jumi gulped. A black-and-white photo hung over Walt's dorm entrance. Walt & Co. mugging before a studio brick wall graffitied *Homies Forever.* Jumi stared at the mock pouts, crossed arms, and turned to the bedroom doors. Each one locked, kids hunched over moral imperative, supply and demand, identity politics. Jumi walked out to the elevator and jammed the button. "Did you take that photo when you visited me?" Walt strolled barefoot behind her. "Probably. Why?" She placed her hand on his thumping chest. "I need to think." "Please," he said, his lower lip trembling, "don't think." The parting doors halved their image to zip.

"So now you know," Vero said when Jumi slumped onto their papasan. "Get used to it or get out." A Santurce doctor's daughter, Vero had started seeing a Colombian lifeguard. Every evening Camus pressed their elevator button, dorm proctors asked for his ID. Vero repeated what he'd said when she'd shrugged. *How would you like it? How would you feel?* But when Jumi rang Walt—*what if her homegirls had snapped themselves in polo shirts before his golf course?*—Walt stammered words that hadn't shown up on her SAT. "It wasn't my prerogative. I merely acquiesced." Jumi asked for her keys. Walt shuffled over. Heads downcast on the church steps.

Jumi whirled about the stage for ten days, knocking over larger girls, the rickety set. When she trudged home from Auburn Street, she found his phone messages like campaign slogans. *We can make it through this! I believe in our future! Give change a chance!* The afternoon she threw up green water in the dressing room, the other Indian girls squealed and pinched their noses. Jumi bolted to Walt's suite—his crushing hug, soapy scent, crowing laugh. When she rolled over, there was the photo, adorning the door.

All year, he bussed to her room instead.

DEEWANA

But my summer nights! Walt slipped from midtown bars and read Styron on the Uptown 5. In a studio that overlooked swaying maples, Jumi YouTubed dance clips till Walt stumbled in. All beer-and-soapy sweetness.

His favorite treat? Her striptease, when she slipped off the back-wagon of her jeans and swiveled to some hip-hop top forty. *Play, repeat.* Her favorite style? Doggy style, when he grabbed every supple orb and growled *mine.* They did the deed atop her quilted radiator, her one dollar chair, the cot under her dead mother's shawl. The cot-the shawl-cot-shawl-cotshawlcotshawlcotshawl. He grew into a mangy wolf, licking at her to *get up, get down,* to stand and walk on him. Acrobatics that turned her into a tightroping swan.

When they stood newborn before the mirror, she said, "We look different." His swimmer's body, all shoulder and leg, had the Nordic height of Punjab, the lithe lines of Chinese script. Her gymnast's body, called childlike, had the sturdy look she'd found in books like "The Tribal People of India." When she tried turning to the cot, he caught her waist. *We're flawless.*

The last evening rain broke the summer heat, he drew her close in the cot. "What would you say if I said"—the maples swished—"I couldn't imagine my life without you?" She pushed him to the wall. "I love you but I'm not in love with you." He pulled her in again. "Give me time. How come," and he lifted the covers into a tent, "this feels so natural?" "Because," she said to the moon gleaming through the sheet, "all lovers live in caves."

By day, they roamed biryani joints in Jackson Heights, El Rey eats in the North Bronx. Though after molé at Grand Concourse, he slumped onto a bench, gazed about the glassy lots, the singed brick. "I can't kiss you here. I've never seen so much poverty." Though after samosa chaat on Roosevelt Avenue, she let go of his hand. Stragglers sang Bollywood tunes she, if not he, understood: *I saw you and I knew, beloved, love is crazy, beloved.*

The crowd crushed them onto trains to his brother's pad. Their fists shifted up and down a metal pole that reflected their bashful glances, while a raven-haired woman watched with knowing eyes. From the Times Square penthouse, Jumi peered at the sparkle of cabs, tourists, billboards, then turned to the spotless coterie of lawyers-bankers-politicians. *Pretty money,* she thought sourly while downing cups of pink champagne. Until Walt led her to a hookah room of pale, shirtless boys, and placed her hand in the slack hand of his brother. Chris sucked at the hookah pipe. "Jumi is Assamese," Walt said, pulling the corners of his eyes out. "Where," Chris puffed in. "Is," he puffed out. "That?"

THE FALL

Cambridge rang—bells under church spires, girls clopping in boots—of crisp, crisp money. Walt and Jumi held hands and cowered under the Harvard Yard arch. Real ivy on old brick! That tiled path that made a suggestive ring! Clean-cut students lugged suitcases in and out dorms, and Jumi stiffened. "I don't know if I'mma make it through this." Walt scanned the tweeds and convertibles of Massachusetts Avenue. "We won't let this tear us apart." After dragging boxes to opposite ends of campus, they made frantic love on her cot.

The news shot through the halls: *Walt and Jumi sitting in a tree, k-i-s-s-i-n-g* . . . . Girls who'd never seen Jumi, who wore Dolce and Prada to class, who rated boys on their Earning Potential, stopped by her room. *My mother would shower me with diamonds.* Boys who'd scoped Jumi out as *pretty but unfriendly,* who bristled at her scornful laugh, who edged near her at parties, picked up her books.

Walt's the nicest guy at school. Rani, a Bengali sylph whose waterfall hair snared as many Indian boys as med school did, shouted over her vacuum cleaner. "If this ends, everyone will blame you!" Bruce, a Chinese Renaissance man whose killer cheekbones sent the Asian girls swooning, announced on a jog, "Dude, it's *Pride and Prejudice* meets *Love Story.*" Vero, who'd warned that the prepsters wanted to "pluck a wildflower," "tame a colt," folded towels gently. "Walt this, Walt that. You know you're allowed to see other boys, right? But *por el amor de Dios*, stop flirting with the ladies." Rajiv, a BJP economist who'd grown a mustache that made him look like Mussolini, noted in section, "Brother, we thought she was half-*Latin*. Not only does she live with *negroes*, she flirts with *ladies.*"

Walt tried to slip them to the ducks and trees of the Commons, but Boston drizzled into gloom. To his house for Mom and pork fried rice, but Jumi slunk about the Russian dolls. The easiest days were nights, when he slung his bookbag over her chair, and she dreamt them back to the Cape. He had pulled over by the dunes, seagrass curtaining the whales, and had thrown their coats over the windows, her orange bikini swinging from the dashboard. They fucked against stenched leather seats, the glass fogging, fogging against creamy birches which shivered as if, any second, a cop might jolt out.

THE STRANGER

Veronica María Alejandra Sánchez had hoofed to Annenberg as a Victoria's Secret Angel: black lace lingerie under red chemise, crepe wings wired to bra latch. The hall teemed with ghouls and devils drinking beer and brandy under stained glass scholars and poets. Vero had been twirling her hands in the air to "Thriller" when someone tapped her shoulder. A Guy-Fawkes-masked man in a Dracula cape looked her up and down, offered his bejeweled gloved hand. *Pero sí tu eres la angel más bonita aquí.* She stumbled home at dawn, holding the 609 digits of Alberto Camus.

Jumi looked askance when Camus plopped on their papasan, but had to admit that those hazel eyes, close-cropped kinks, and that roguish laugh that made him tramp to Vero's princess. Jumi hadn't expected Vero's taste, but then, Vero didn't know why Jumi stuck it out with Type As. Camus, finding himself in The Towers, worked the crowd. He parodied bowtied Harvard boys, sang Knight Rider bhangra by heart, replaced Jumi's tangled bike chain. Each time he brought Vero burritos, he left chocolates on Jumi's cot. The Sunday my girls hauled laundry to the basement, Jumi said, "He's smart. He knows the way to a woman's yoni is through her friends."

LIFE OF SIN

I'd say, Thanksgiving night, his uncles ushered Walt into the study and asked when he was going to marry Jumi. His brother, scanning her wild curls over the disemboweled turkey, said Walt would raise pygmies. His parents, setting out plates of pumpkin pie, asked for a number, but when Jumi said kids would end her career, Walt raised three cream-topped fingers. Yet who could say *nay* in that holly-hung house, by photo-framed fireplaces? Jumi, pooped from class-dance-scholarship chores, crashed and snored like a motorcycle in a room strewn with toy boats, postered with exquisite maps. Walt shuffled over with dewy eyes, then lay rubbing his paunch, crooning "Bonnie and Clyde," till intoning over her lips, *my girlfriend.*

Boston would say, but the girl considered other men. Not white boys who hooted *Jumi from the block*, but dusky boys who rambled shyly about Marx over dining hall soup. "You don't always gotta bring up Walt," she told one brother, who watched the bangles clink on her wrists. She even listened to pudgy aunties who tackled her in the wings, asked her age-caste-major, named which *so good-looking son* would be starting *vaat six-figure salary.* Right in front of Walt, who said nothing.

We'd both say, Vero tossed and turned across the hall. Camus's hazel eyes turned out to be magnets for any kind of pretty. After choir one evening, Vero collapsed on the papasan and talked a mile a minute about which guy had catcalled or winked at her. Jumi stopped typing. "Why are you dressed like you are going to a funeral? You know you like color." Vero flung her peacoat off and a tear eeled down her cheek. "Alberto hooked up with his ex." Jumi gasped and knelt by Vero. "Lose the mofo. He knows he's not in your league." Vero gazed at the ceiling. "I'm not upset. He's ending things with her." Jumi slid back. "Veronica, do you believe him?" Vero gave a tight smile. "Chica, I wish we all had the same luck. *Pero así es la vida.*"

Our Future

At P.F. Chang's, Vero folded and refolded her napkin as Walt and Jumi hissed. The baby-faced waitress hovered close, then drew back. Was Eminem famous because he was pink? Was Monica Belucci the most beautiful woman because she was white? What sort of Desi called England the Mother Country?

"You're colonized," Jumi cried over spring rolls. "A banana, a coconut, a twinkie, a-a-a . . ."

"Stop being so pedantic," Walt snapped. "You're boring everyone."

The genteel old couple next to them, who had not paid for this Christmas entertainment, drank their soups worriedly. *Slurp, slurp. This is our future. Slurp, slurp.* Each couple looked forlornly at the other.

Yet New Year's Eve, Walt held Jumi's hand down the glowing corridor of Faneuil Hall. He pointed out gleaming stalls of lobster and sushi, creamy barrels of chowder and gelato. Snow melted off Jumi's dark coat. They strolled until they reached the rotunda, where Vero and Camus giggled and chewed corn cobs on a bench. Walt and Jumi unclasped hands.

"That's weird," Jumi said. "I told her we were coming here for our six-month anniversary."

"Great," Walt said. "An evening with Dopey."

The four kids made small talk in the spotlight of the rotunda: *Fuckin' ey! What the—? Tan loco!* Camus, who'd heard of this Other Boyfriend for months, challenged Walt to an eating contest. Walt wrinkled his nose and looked off at the newsstand, but Camus tucked in his Che T-shirt and zipped through ten cobs. He pumped his fists—the girls laughed—Walt plucked his molar with a toothpick. On the Hall's marble steps, kids sliding down the slopes on boards, Camus pelted Walt with snowballs. The girls turned away to cheer on the snowboarders while Walt darted and dodged from Camus. "Here, pussy-pussy-pussy," Camus cried. Walt glowered behind a garbage can.

Later, Jumi toweled Walt down in her bathroom. "That's just his way," she said. Walt punched the shower door. "I'm not hanging out with them again." Jumi yanked the towel away. "I hang out with your friend who calls turban-wearers 'towelheads.'" Walt pulled on his boxers and marched out the door. "So don't. But at least I don't alienate the Indians here." Jumi followed his wet footprints to her room. "Are you serious? You're taking cover behind those kiss-asses?"

Cartoons of Apu, quotes by Gandhi had floated, a year after 9/11, like flags across stately buildings. *Get to know your friendly neighborhood Indian*, the fliers read. *Free samosas*. Indian couples in black peacoats walked gingerly about The Yard, faces clouded with the gloom wafting over the country. On the SAA LISTSERV, folks spelled out Dotbusters, shootings in Texas, clubbings in New York, and said, *We may need to go to war*. Jumi half-joked back, *Do we really want to play good Indian, bad Indian*, and the LISTSERV had shot back, *high horse, traitor, leftie!*

Jumi hugged Walt, who frowned out the window at the murky river, and said, "They say hi to you now and completely ignore me." He turned around and rewrapped Jumi's towel around her hips. "Sometimes, it's better not to say anything. We don't always have to agree. You don't have to take everything to heart."

GAME

After she'd stroked his scar a hundred times, Walt confessed to Jumi. He hadn't thought any woman would want him. His foreskin had wrapped so tightly over his broad tip, he'd pulled back the flap to pee. He'd funked through high school until his father cornered him by the ferns. Only after surgery did Walt chat up a cheerleader. "That's why," he grinned, "I've got so much game." Jumi grunted.

"Your game is zero game."

Jumi screwed her windows against the first frost and crawled under a quilt. *She'd never planned a wedding.* Too much time at bus stops with sixteen-year-olds and their babies. At the restaurant with Punjabis and whities licking their lips. Sure, she'd mooned at boys in class—cream-and-honey-and-coffee-skinned boys—but who looked at a nerdy flaca? "Bronx boys," she muttered into Walt's chest, "may be the most beautiful boys in the world. But they're also the rudest."

Vero was more romantic than Valentine's Day. She trolled wedding sites for dresses with Princess Di trains, for venue dates at El Rincón. She teared up when repeating The Legend of Camus: how he'd hitchhiked from Colombia to Mexico, been smuggled on a donkey cart here, sent money for his brother's schooling.

"Are you sure your parents will like him?" Jumi said.

Vero shrugged. "My dad picked my mom from a chorus line. What's he gonna say?"

"Doesn't Alberto worry?" Jumi said.

Vero snapped her chocolate bar and gave Jumi half. "Alberto says, 'if you can do something, why worry? If you can't, why worry?'"

No one told them about the memory of places. How even the river, waiting-waiting, would gurgle up a thousand-year warning. That land and loss are constant. That forgiveness is the hardest trick of all.

Dogs

Maybe it began the March night she swept the glass animals he'd gifted her off her desk. They smashed into shards so luminescent, she wanted to roll about in them. Rise armored with colored glass. He froze at her laptop, where he'd been clicking on a game. She *hated* how he was the popular one, just 'cause he was some rich kid? He knelt by her cot and sobbed. "You don't know how I feel about you." She crackled onto the glass. "No one knows how you feel about anything." He wanted to bash her dark eyes in. Wasn't she the one who wept in closets? *Homesick, scholarship kid, cold-ass town.* Yet he'd soap her down, toast cheese sandwiches, watch *I Love Lucy* clips till she uncoiled. He spread his arms. "Doesn't it mean something that you push but I stay put?"

Maybe it was the evening he thumped shampoo into her scalp and muttered. *His boys had caught her talking to the dance professor.* She slammed off the knob. Stalked dripping to her room. *Was she under surveillance?* He tried to draw her in by the mirror. "Calm down! You're yapping like a Chihuahua!" She jerked away and yanked open drawers. *Did he think they were the prince and the pauper? At least the prof wasn't a stuck-up . . .* he kicked the soccer ball at her ankles. "I get it! You people are the unsung dogs of Asia!" The ball bounced off the drawer and struck the mirror. Teetering . . . toppling . . . smash! Their startled faces scattered over the floor.

Their fingers bled as they picked up the jagged pieces.

"My mom picked my dad because he had I-N-T-E-G-R-I-T-Y!"

"Your mom's dead! Stop romanticizing the past!"

"At least I don't worship whiteness!"

"At least I don't follow made-up gods!"

Walt dumped glass into the bin and jabbed the message button on her answering machine. The voice of her high school buddy graveled out: "I probably shouldn't say this, it being Valentine's Day and all . . . but oy gevalt! I fucked a girl today! I felt like the President conquering China."

Jumi shivered on the floor. Walt yanked the cord from the socket. "How the hell do you call me a dog and not him?"

Maybe it was the nights after, the funk between them turning their bed ballet into half-hearted hop. He couldn't get it up as much—"You've lost so much weight," he cried as he crushed her under him—she got off only one way now—facing away from him, cowgirl style, longing for trees that trembled up branches. Would they, she gasped, bloom?

She asked Vero a few hours after she walked in on her, topless and giddy, under Camus. Vero slipped on her glasses and sat back in the papasan like a therapist. "Just come out and tell him, Jumi. I. Need. More. Lovin'." Camus leapt between the girls and pinned Vero back onto the cushion. "Just say, lemme show you how it's done." Vero clasped Camus securely as he settled onto her lap, and Jumi squinted past them, into the dark, where sakura buds were curled against the frost.

LOVE ALONE

The day they dropped theses into boxes, ice slithered off roofs. Thawed the Charles into sludge. But Jumi, riding the T for hours, wept in Chinatown and couldn't say why. Not even to the black man who sat on her bench and said, "Is it that bad?" When she kept sobbing, he said, "Now, now. It'll pass." Several minutes later, "I better go before I get arrested. You take care."

Walt sipped coffee in the sun-dappled Square and tracked the wind. Boys hurling Frisbees, girls lingering in dresses. On his lap, purple orchids for Jumi. Under his loafers, sharp cobblestones. Over his head, the sudden, open sky.

They slept back to back and browsed work sites secretly. Till the breezy morning Jumi poured him a cup of bitter Assam. "Can you believe it? Dancing in the foothills for a year!" Walt scalded his tongue and stared out her window. The Charles churning, churning. "You wanna live in la-la-land." Jumi hugged his head. "Visit me. I promise you'll like it."

The few times they slept together, they woke with one kid sprawled on the floor.

"What did you expect?" Vero said. She tiptoed to a tin of condensed milk on the shelf. "You're so skittish." Jumi rubbed her temples. "I'm so tired I can't think straight." Vero frowned at the tin. "This turns to dulce de leche at home." She shoved it back. "You *pick*. Por ejemplo, I get tired of listening to Alberto talk about electronics and sports. But he makes me laugh. He's devoted. And *he* gets sick of all *this*." Jumi kicked the soccer ball. "For real?" Vero paused the ball. "I got a research grant to Peru. We're talking about phone calls, visits, the whole deal."

When Jumi brought up Camus, Walt stabbed his dining hall pudding. Jumi pulled out the knife. "Forget India! Your friends think I'm lucky you visit the Bronx!" Five jock girls slid to the table's other end. "I bought a plane ticket already, okay?" Walt said. "I'm teaching near your home next year, got it?" Jumi scraped back her chair. The Azores ladies in their hairnets were wiping down tables, listening in. They had told Jumi: Walt was bonito, he would be rico, she could dance por sempre. Walt cupped her face. "Throw me a bone, Jumi. No one can live on love alone."

ETA TIERRA

Graduation day, the Sanchezes flew up—*ay que frío eta tierra*—and cheered in The Yard. Vero had marched to the front row, right on time, but Jumi, who had woken up late, trailed the last file to the back. She looked around for her father's small stature, stern face— *kot asa Baba?*—but it was Camus who clapped her eyes *gotcha!* from behind. After the Latin speeches, the English speeches that sounded Latin, my kids trooped back to change into jeans. Camus, cornering Mr. Sanchez by the papasan, rapped his favorite song about big ol' booties by good ol' Mix-A-Lot . . . a normally beaming dentist, Mr. Sanchez clutched his belly as if in labor.

Mr. Saikia met them at Pho Pasteur, where he shot Walt dirty glances over the menu. Walt gorged on vermicelli as if it were his pre-execution meal. Mr. Sanchez happily overpowered the silences with tales of his yacht. The hour—Walt's brother talking to Mr. Saikia as if one of them were retarded, Camus downing beer as if he'd found an oasis, Jumi explaining for the nth time *this dance in a war zone thing*—ended on the restaurant threshold. Brattle Street, where the kids had skidded over so much icy doubt, was a glittering curlicue of stone. As the Sanchezes chattered about airport shuttles, Mr. Saikia turned into a bitter wind, which tossed Jumi's words over the Singhs' guarded faces. "See you soon?"

Walt was left standing alone, gazing from one tide of backs to another.

Double-Fault

She summered on Orchard Beach, watching the elliptical dips of the gulls. When some island guy came up to even her skinny ass—blunt stare, cajoling talk—she flirted till shutting down into a book. "Ninety-nine percent of the time," she told Vero on a visit, "I'm on top. Is that normal?"

"How about it's sweet?" Vero said, slipping on her sunglasses. In her Yankees T-shirt and cutoffs, Vero drew glances to her guitar hips, her cavalier recline. "Ay chica." She rose and shook off sand. "Stop kicking him to the curb. Decide and be done with it." She strolled to the sea rim and rung Camus.

August. A gold-skinned pão sauntered up as she lay reading *Strangers of the Mist*. He asked for the bathroom in mangled Spanish—she gazed around at the vast sand and bush—he grinned. They spent the day pacing the strip, comparing notes on Nova Iorque, capoeira, goddesses. He told her his grandmother was an Indian and belted orixa songs at the sea. They drove to City Island, where they shared fried calamari and tossed fries up to the frenzied gulls. At dusk, they parted on the Island Bridge, the Brazilian blushing at Jumi's eager lips.

August. Walt smoked blunts with his brother. Cruised downtown with his buddies. Ogled strippers with creamy tits, endless legs. Hit tennis balls with The Other Asian, Scott Lee, a Korean frog about half Walt's height and color. The very last game, Walt called Jumi.

"I don't know what happened!"

She set her basket of sandy clothes on the washing machine.

"I had him. Two sets up, a break in the third. Then my knees buckled. I sank right there on the court. When I got up, I was a different man."

Jumi dumped the clothes and slammed the lid. "We all lose sometimes."

"You're not listening!" Walt cried. "I kept double-faulting, hitting easy balls out. He demolished me."

Chug-a-lug the machine thrummed. "Next time," she said. "We can't always get what we want."

"I can't believe it," he whispered. "I can't believe I lost."

THE MOON

If India was another planet, the Northeast was its moon.

Jumi danced weekly on makeshift stages, in Guwahati fields, Naga villages, Shillong churches. The ruddy cheeks, brushstroke eyes made her want to pull Walt through the phone. "You would fit in here!" But their phone connections were so fuzzy that Walt only heard half her sentences. "We cancelled the tour to Imphal last minute because of a bomb blast," she said. He heard, "We tour Imphal last because it's a blast!" When he called the Imphal hotel with card after card he'd bought in Indian groceries, the receptionist giggled, "Hasta la vista, baby!" Jumi, eating momos in a Kohima hotel, fell asleep to the cop flick *Paap*.

"Family obligations," Walt said for Diwali and stayed in Massa-chussetts. Jumi rattled on a Jeep to Kanchenjunga, a crisp blue peak that marked the Old Silk Road. Her travel mates, boisterous Benga-lis who swapped tiffins of fish curry and rasmalai, cheerily informed her she was a typical backward Northeasterner. She clutched the door as they zipped around misty hill passes and prayed for life, lib-erty, and the pursuit of peace. But at the Gangtok Monastery, Jumi wandered the red halls and felt her gut surge. She wanted to ruin every shaven monk who strolled by: spare faces, maroon robes with flame shirts peeking through. She shitted so long over holes she thought she'd grown new thigh muscles, stopped shielding her rear from men who leered. "Ah, sexy, sexy shit!"

Then, at an Arunachali dance performance, she met a prince. A punk rock-loving, Johnny Walker-drinking prince who invited her to museums, parks, cafes. Who steered her and his hounds in a Jeep along the lush riverbank, across cow-ridden bridges, past elephants lumbering from forests. Who sang full-throttle to Bob Dylan, who slapped his knees at goofy jokes, who studied Jumi sideways as if she were a marvelous alien visiting his planet. It struck her later as an old-fashioned courtship—whole villages watching, whispering— that fizzled out. Because she had to tour; because she'd be gone; because Walt called every Friday. *I miss you*s and *what's new*s that left her dizzy. "Why do you sound so weird?" he said. "I'm sorry," she said.

Mostly, the moon made her gasp. Emerald hills capped by clouds. Girls click-clacking striped shawls on looms. Blackouts when folks lit kerosene lamps and spoke. Names that belonged to the jobless and the junkies, the fighters and the fucked who crouched at town edges. The names weighed on Jumi as she danced, so that she felt like a puppet. The dances themselves, once rich with twirl, seemed desperate. Or, as two French tourists put it, "*so* simple an animal could do them."

FAT KID LOVE

Walt's parents stared at the crooked streets, bargain stores, shambled tracks, and said, "Parkchester looks like a war zone." Indeed, those first brutal months, the kids stampeded over *Mr. S*. Kids who seemed more invested in Dungeons & Dragons than in the Constitution. Who said basketball was more practical than the UN? Who remembered mack lines—*mami, you so fine you make a n——God whine*—rather than his PowerPoint words—*decorum, restraint*. Who didn't know what to make of Mr. S: Pancake Face, Ching Chong, Tiger Woods? Walt pointed to his brown forearm and said, "See? I'm also Indian." The kids neck-bobbed about the classroom, slapping their mouths in war chants.

"Welcome to my childhood," Jumi said.

For Christmas, she broke up with him. The thirtieth time. He zombied through the American Civil War, then graded till bedtime. When he couldn't sleep, he drank vodka shots and jogged to Jumi's parkway. Heaved on a bench till a crackhead, rising-falling, asked for change. When she called him a month later, pleading for one more chance, he sighed. "Jumi, I can't play this game anymore." When she yelled at him about his spoiled ways, he yelled back that he'd known she'd regret it. "Fine," they cried. "I'm over it!"

Then there were days the children sprang forth like llamas. Little blond Nathan punched him in the hallway. *This too shall pass. L'chaim!* Little Boricua Miriam pulled him down by his tie. *Cheer up. You could die.* Days when rap became a revelation: the rhythms that sounded like trains, the monotone delivery that unfolded into witness, the surprisingly rosy-and-blue ballads. Why Jumi had said 50 Cent had penned the world's most romantic lines, lines he'd half-heard when she called him *sweet cake*, lines he overheard his kids singing daily to each other. *I love you*, they shouted. *I love you*, they drooled. *I love you*, they prayed. Why he saw with sudden clarity masks drop from faces. Who parented parents; who got locked in basements; who, no matter what, would run through the cracks.

He lay on his bed, listening to the number four rumble by, and a seismic shift shot through him. He couldn't even save himself.

BURNT

Their last supper at Kebab King, he told Jumi about the Austrian girl. A teacher who had drunkenly admired his exotic skin, exotic lips, exotic eyes. Who didn't have Jumi's hang-ups: brown girl secrecy, self-loathing, rage. Who was twice as beautiful, twice as troubled, twice as worldly. "I don't know why she chose me," he said, frowning at the calamari. Jumi patted his shoulder. "She has good taste." He jerked back and scowled at her hand. "You look burnt."

They tried talking on the phone, as he plowed through his last teaching year and she danced at a Jersey theater. But when he yelled about the time and money he'd wasted on her, how he was better than ninety-nine percent of dogs she'd meet, she said nothing. Later, she wept before the mirror. Her dark skin! Her tiny limbs! Her broke ass! Her father drove those evenings from the restaurant, a routine that grayed his hair. "You are my blood, you are my heart, you are my star," he bent over her. But she couldn't hear any of it.

She cut Walt off and danced like a madwoman. He checked in with friends who'd attended her shows: how did she look? Was she with someone? He gave her email to girls who'd gossiped about her, who suddenly wanted to befriend them both. He left a voicemail rant, saying he was "appalled and disgusted" she'd slept with his Korean friend. She considered telling him Mr. Do-Gooder had hidden her from his church friends, had a pecker the size of a pinky, which explained his pious airs. She called to say, "You think your name is stamped on my forehead? How many girls have you slept with?" Walt snapped, "if you act like a kindergartener, I'll treat you like one," then hung up.

She called once more, the night her father lay in the ICU. She sat on a stool, every jump of the heart monitor kicking her own guts, and said, "What if he dies?" Walt could only talk about cheating on Anna, about how he and Jumi got derailed, about how, years later, they might've worked. "Are you listening?" Jumi asked and Walt cried, "I'm talking for once! It's your job to listen!" After she gently pressed the receiver, she counted how many times the pump by her father's head sent air into his lungs, the plastic bag of blood by his feet circled in and out his sides. She touched the veins spidering over his wrists as snappable as hers. *Deeta, can you hear me?*

GALAXIES
Years later, she'd spot in strangers his gentle hunch and squint harder to reel him in. Luminous planets spinning. Years later, he'd call three more times, alternately yelling and weeping. *If I could do it again, I'd do it differently.* Years later, she'd be coaching wild-limbed girls, and he'd mirage from a chair in the back. Dwarf suns throbbing. Years later, he'd hear from some law crony, over lobster bisque, how much she'd given up! *Not just him but propriety.*

He didn't hear how, the afternoon Vero and Camus traded rings, Jumi walked to that bridge over the Charles. How a bagpiper blared a ditty that had roused them each dawn. How she wasn't ready for the tears that sprang up when longboats rowed into the light.

Swan Lake Tango

We're together tonight, Sammy standing right behind me, and still, I want to run down and touch him, my other guy. Chandeliers glitz the lobby, doors open like mouths, and there he is among the black coats. Isn't it him: Walter Singh? Shoulders sloping with prep school ease? Sweaters and slacks made for wineglass company I've never kept, never will?

Girls like me, who want to make with boys like him, hate ourselves for it, but want it every time. We want to press our fingers between those blades, so those brown eyes feel without shifting, the fundamental message. *Walt, it's Jumi. Your first. Love-love-love.*

But Sammy's hand, my wrist, saves me from the coats, and that shiny head—an ordinary face—poof! melts into crowd.

"Everything okay?" Sammy says.

"Perfect," I say, hugging him, praying, *please don't let me fuck this up, let me keep this, let me pretend.*

We fold away our usher gloves, hold sweaty hands out into Lincoln Center Plaza—and what do you know? I look for Walt. Here on the street, the starless sky over us, the city lights blurring figures rushing by, I squeeze Sammy's hand. I clasp two men in one body, I meld past and present, I make amends.

Sam, don't tell me magic ain't real. If your heart's anything like mine, it can pull some pretty screwy shit.

⤺

Odile, the black swan, swirls only into Tchaikovsky's third act, to steal the prince from the rightful swan, the white one. I imagine her on thick Russian legs once favored by critics, fluttering her talons for the kill. I imagine her pirouetting her glossy black tail, as if to say, *Why choose goodness when you can fling me up, born of ambition and bitterness and my father's tricks?*

⤺

At dawn, I hop the train to reach the studio first, even before Sammy, and dance the tango alone. It's a tricky dance, this tussle between lovers, and I still don't have the beat down. Sure, *slide*-step-step, but your partner's *supposed* to change the sequence on you. That's why you've got to hold the beat, you've got to have rhythm, something nobody can teach you.

Another pair of ears, a separate beating heart, arms and legs that cut the stage to their own sweet minutes—and rhythm's near impossible. I figure I might as well dance alone, but the teachers say I'd have to imagine someone in order to learn. And I don't know anymore who I'd pick, what I want, how much distance to keep. I don't know if any tango is worth it.

After all, the teachers also say movement never lies, it's the barometer of the soul. Well then, how come I couldn't tell Walt would waltz me into a scary corner? Why can't I say if, after one tender reggae, Sammy and I are going to sit the rest of this out?

⤺

Maybe I should've seen the signs, like those end-of-relationship mornings when Sammy fetal-curled in his sleep, warding off my memories, or when I started thinking back to why things ended for Walt and me.

"I can't take it anymore," Walt had said. "There's a limit to how much anyone can take. Maybe I've reached mine."

Twenty-seven times I'd dumped him, and always we'd reached for each other again, in his dorm room or mine. Our crazy-in-love act had spoiled me.

"Don't you care anymore?" I said.

Girls drifted by our Cambridge bench like Chanel and Gucci models.

"Jumi," he said. "Jumi, I don't know."

But Sammy knew the day we paired in the *axé*, the moment he held my wrist and spun me. He let me know back, with his up-down flicking eyes, his nervous talk of Graham over coffee, his silver Corolla pulled right on time for dinner at Siam King.

"I've never felt this way," he said the first night, his torso an ivory tusk under a fat Bronx moon.

"You're just a baby," I said, and rubbed my toe up his dolphin limbs.

He is twenty-two, younger than I was when Walt and I stopped talking, and as white as the early morning paper. Lord have mercy, is what all the aunties are thinking. *Jumi, have fun. Jumi, don't get attached. Jumi, does he do it like an Indian?*

My baby does it like a man. Maybe it was the fake sex that did me and Walter in, how he lay there like a virgin, not knowing push or pull of his God-given gift, waiting for me to strut and work myself on top. Did rich boys need a tutor for loving? Or did they slum to break themselves in, then move on up the ladder?

When Walter became a man, it was with some Heidi and Laura after me, and he said delectably, like he was sucking on a cherry, "You could say the white woman's been the ghost in my relationships."

(No, asshole, I wouldn't.)

And just like that—snap!—my heart a thin brown twig.

Sammy wouldn't say it. Sammy says nothing, like a good white boy, till too late. Only once, with my bronze limbs crossed over his pale pink chest, did he say, "The color of my true love's hair is black."

It's the Irish poet in him that won me over, and the Irish drunk that tries to turn me out. Eight months of him laughing and snoring, eight months of me crying and yelling—and still, I won't give up. Off the sheet between me and Sammy, Walt shimmers and croons. *Jumi, you don't have what it takes. Jumi, you don't know what compromise means. Jumi, are you going to fuck this up as well?*

"We're too different," Sammy tells the ceiling.

"That," I answer, "was visible from the start."

Then I roll over and say what Walt said a hundred times, proving to Sammy that his Catholic miracles are real, or to myself that karma's a bitch. "Give me one more chance. I can change."

↩

Black Swan (n). *A rare sub-species with black coloring once considered a genetic impossibility.*

The Tango (n). *Lover's duel, believed to have originated with freed slaves and danced between men.*

A Lake (n). *An enclosed body of water; a place to fish or drown; a meeting point in Swan Lake, where characters fall in love, morph, and die.*

↩

Playtime's over, the troupe trickling into the studio, arching their backs and stretching their calves in sun. Sammy pliés with the men by the brightest pole and doesn't look over, doesn't say hi, plays hot and cold like a true tango dancer. Sometimes, I think he's too dedicated to his craft. I know we should feel *la alma de tango* and all, but that doesn't entail being a deaf-and-dumb dick.

A cello worms sadly into the air, and I clippity-clop over and say, "Morning, baby."

"Morning," he says.

"I left early to warm up," I say.

"Okay," he says. "So did I."

On the honey floor, dancers shuffle into pairs, bodies slanted like arrows aimed at the sky.

"Come on," I say, placing his hand on my waist, reciting from the postcard on the studio door. "Let's make a date . . ."

Slide-step-step.

" . . . to tango quite late."

Sammy pauses me, shifts us left. "And when we get tired . . ." he says.

Slide-step-step.

" . . . we'll just hesitate."

But he won't look at me and he doesn't sound sure.

❧

Since the Caitlin thing, Sammy and I are working on what he calls "space," what feels to me like an abyss he's dropped into, off a cliff he pulled me to in the first place. Already one month, but his sweatshirts and condoms still lie around, and the one weekend night he comes to claim something, we play Boggle instead.

Always, I lose. I'm not skilled at teasing points from plurals, reading backward, or jumbling words up. Always, we switch to another game, what he calls my mother country legacy: I've got hope, he's got the diamond, and we make like a luxury item neither of us can afford. When he sweats over me, I tell him I love his fucking jewels, I love a guy like him.

Truth is, I do, but I also hate the rich, the way they parade their wants, junk what they've used, how they can't fathom any suffering other than theirs.

"How could you do this?" I said when he first said "space," right after he'd come back from Texas, where his rich redneck daddy lives, and his beer-guzzling ex, Caitlin. I threw a bottle past him, shattering it into confetti on his bed. "I *trusted* you. And look where it got me!"

Sammy held his head. "Like a trained dog, the past rolls over to die, then pounces on you from behind."

"What did you say?"

"*You* said that. One of those times babbling about Walter."

"I said it because I didn't want to repeat it."

But from the start, we were counting our ghosts.

At dinner, when Sammy rose for the toilet, his daddy said, "What do your folks do? What part of the city they from?" After his daddy left, Sammy said, "He asked if I really like the ethnic type. And said you spoke good English." When Sammy called it quits, my father said, "These Americans. For them, it's easy come, easy go. No understanding of commitment."

So I lie in my empty bed, the wind howling through the winter branches, and wonder if Walter was right. I'll never find a guy as good as him; I'll never work it out with anyone else; no one's man enough for me.

I lie in bed, my heart pumping the way it did the night Caitlin called, one month ago.

"Sammy, I love you," she screamed. "I've always loved you, I always will."

"Drunk-dial," Sammy told me.

And I lay in bed, stark brown naked, telling him I didn't like such things one bit. And when he rose to leave, telling him I didn't mind it from him, I minded it from her. And when he gripped the doorknob to shut it, telling him space was good, space would calm us down, things were mostly fine, we could work things out.

❧

Dancing again and again into your lover's heart is no joke when it is as hyped as Texas and you are as jittery as the Bronx and the dance is far-off Argentinean, so standing still seems safer because you are prima donna at running, having long vaulted out the nosebleed section for Love in the front row, except you've met the Bad Boy you always outran in this Greco-Roman cowboy who measures out spiced spaghetti sauce from his Grandma's Scratch before he lures you with gringo Spanish into an unmade bed, and before he backs up, spur-step by spur-step, out the door, scuffed black shoes cocked straight at your heart.

ᴗ

Water break—and as dancers part, Sammy drops me and rushes to the pole. I trail after him, and when I touch his shoulder, the other guys turn to watch.

"After you left last night," I say, "I called several times."

"I turned off my phone," he says.

For whom, I want to ask, but maybe I know already and maybe it doesn't really matter. The cello's wailing again, and when Sammy steers us back to the center, we don't look at each other. We take our stances like two prizefighters, and I assess the men I could have danced with instead.

Allen Mackenzie: Mr. Goldilocks in a red ruffled shirt, prancing like some frisky Clydesdale horse. Ryan Leung: Asian flexmaster with his crazy turns, his face stern like he'd murder you if he had the time. Jason Stackhouse: black Jesus with his outstretched arms, his eyes fixed either up at the disco ball or down on the floor.

I guess I'm lucky, but still. I strain against Sammy when he pushes. I pull away when he would turn.

"What are you doing?" he says.

"Dancing," I say. "Same as you."

He dips me then, and because I stare upside down at the next couple, I almost slip.

"If you don't want to dance," he says, "just say so."

"I want to dance," I say. "I want to talk straight with you."

"I don't feel like we can do that anymore," he says.

"Which?" I ask. "Wait," I say as he walks like an injured king to that pole. "Where are you going?" I call, running with him down the dingy stairs. "Don't leave," I shout, but he merges into the cab-and-peopled streets.

And there I stand, on the grating in my tango heels, and every face that turns to sneer is Walter's. Polished, wide-eyed, hard. *Surprise, surprise, Jumi. I don't feel sorry for you.*

☙

I told Sammy stories about Walter, maybe too many.

The first few months, I told him how Walter nicknamed me cavewoman, hobbit, bottom-heavy; how when I cried and said he didn't make me feel beautiful, Walter poked my tummy and mimicked me; how when his little man failed, Walter said I didn't dress sexy enough, and when I brought it up again, said *I never said that, you're exaggerating.*

The first few months, Sammy cradled me and whispered, "You don't have to worry with me. I'll never do that."

I told Sammy how, when I got picked as first dancer, Walter said the director was a dirty old man; how Walter would praise this gorgeous girl, but one by one, I had to stop talking to my friends; how when I called Walter, after getting mugged one night, he asked me to call later, his friends were over, the basketball game was about to end.

In our summer fights about his flirting, his drinking, his plans for what we did when, Sammy said, "Please don't compare me to Walter. You've got to trust me."

I told Sammy how Walter's brother called me volatile, because I'd tried breaking up twenty-seven times, and I'd shamefully agreed; how he finally told me, "You'd teach our son Assamese, and I'd want him to be President;" how in the last days, he'd yell at me for hours on the phone.

In the end, when Sammy was coming unannounced at the

house to return my gifts, he said crossly, "I don't even want to hear his name. I'm nothing like him."

I told Sammy how when my father had cancer, Walter never asked how he was doing; how Walter gave out my email to keep tabs on me after I moved; how, when I called him one last time, he said he'd cheated on his girlfriend, and that he and I should get together.

Now Sammy says, as he lies beside me on Boggle nights, and it's this that scares me most: "I don't care if you contact him. Go ahead."

↬

Redemption Moves Like This. When Sammy first brought up classes, he was spinning about the kitchen in just his khakis, one palm over his belly button, another up in the air. Clasping the hand of a woman I couldn't see. "Once upon a time, it was a pimp-prostitute dance," he said. "Born in the slums of Buenos Aires." All I heard was the baleful bandoneon and all I said was "but it looks expensive with those roses and heels and lace." He slid left past the colander and the knives, and I didn't wonder where he'd learned the lines he repeated, "Tango's not in the feet but in the heart." So I hopped down from the barstool and pummeled into his chest—his frown sloshed up like my Singha—but he drew me in, as I later learned you didn't do in tango—*be close yet free*—and misleadingly step-slid us round the kitchen, across the hall, into the living room where we peeled apart on the couch. Arms splayed, feet moist, breathing off-time.

↬

Stupid heels! It's like running the ten blocks to Sammy's apartment on nails, all while trying to think of one good story to convince him.

Maybe I could say how:

My two years with Walt, we danced *twice*. Our first date, he marched his knees up and down, flapped his elbows like wings, grabbed my waist and spun me, howling the words. No rhythm at all, just sheer energy, and I thought *what a sweet, sweet boy.*

Our last dance, he left me on the floor alone, so I hung over the railing, watching him schmooze with his friends, in their neat suits, clinking glasses. I hadn't wanted to witness Harvard kids bopping to rap lyrics they knew nothing about. So I waved for him to take me home, where, with our shadows rocking on the wall, our love-making felt like one of us was dead.

Or I could tell Sammy that:

For a white boy, he has the moves, can salsa and samba with any Carnival king. That's what made me laugh the first time, his serious chin, his flaring nostrils, the way he counted under his breath: *one*-two-three, *one*-two-three, *one*-two-three.

"Those numbers aren't gonna run away," I said.

Flare-flare went his nostrils and he glared at me.

But I had to like a guy who'd try anything, even styles he didn't know, drinking two beers to get himself going, dancing all night to reggaeton he didn't like just to please me.

"Hurray! You scored brownie points," I said.

"Good. That's what I was going for," and he slipped his palms way inside my belt.

But now, when I see my baby packing his bags like a soldier, I say instead, "Sammy. Let's talk at least."

He slumps down onto the bed.

Movement never lies. Is this a ruse of his?

"Let's wait," I say, "for the Christmas show."

"What good will that do?" he says.

I kneel before him and hold his hands.

"We'll have time to cool down and think," I say.

And bless him—he isn't Walt—he can't be—he says like a wary little boy, "I don't know if I can wait that long. But okay."

❧

Tonight's Christmas stage, men leap like stags, fly with the wings of swans, and I track their shadows darting over Sammy's face. He's got the profile of a Roman coin, all angled nobility, not the lush Indian lips, round Chinese nose of Walt, who got called pretty, halfie, a Tiger Woods. All this time I took—two years alone—to pick a different man, and I find someone who'd model Calvin Klein just as easy, fight the hordes just as quick with his stubborn ways, has led too charmed a life to hold my sorrows longer than a hot potato.

"Baby," I begin, and twirl his curls with my finger. But he hunches as if dreading what I might say, and studies the fifteen male torsos bobbing together.

So I pace the stairs with my flashlight and watch other city-dwellers do their dirty deeds. Row E, Korean guy feels his white girlfriend's ass; Row D, two bald black men curl and uncurl their hands and cry; Row B, Dominican girl hugs man on the left, man on the right, stroking each one's cheek. I'm her—the hussy, the tomato in a sandwich, a woman who can't choose between her men, even when one's gone, and the other's getting ready to go.

Act III now, when the black swan flits dangerously into the ball. The Prince, thinking her the enchanted swan princess, draws close to dance. The tempo picks up, the black swan does piqué turn after turn about the Prince, and I run the stairs back to Sammy before it's too late.

"I still love you," I say, just as the Prince embraces the black swan as his wife.

I might as well be telling a ghost, 'cause Sammy stares awhile at the stage, then looks at me with *I'm-sorry-but-I'm-lost-to-you* eyes.

"Don't you love me?" I ask.

"I don't know," he says, "how I feel."

"I don't know," Walt had said. "'Life's a poor player,'" Shakespeare wrote, "'that struts and frets his hour upon the stage.'" Rehearsal goes something like this, I think. You do the same moves over and over, hoping for the moment—voila!—when you get the dance right. Except, fuck-up that I am, I haven't. I haven't yet.

"I'll make changes," I say. "I promise."

Sammy frowns at the Prince as if his pirouettes en pointe are to blame.

"Okay, okay. Don't say anything," I say. "We'll talk about this later. We'll take it one day at a time."

"All right," he says, and because it's *intermezzo*, the lights go out.

∽

Revelation Moves Like That. For fifteen, it's just me and the understudy blinking at the shadowy stage, when I know Sammy's been spelling the truth. I've watched this knobby-legged waif, perched in the orchestra seat, in her Odile variations: the black swan who comes to devastate the party. Her reckless lines, her impossible toes, yet a cold reach in how she will throw back her head, fling up her foot as she claims what every partygoer assumes is Odette's. I don't know her real name but what is real in the theater anyways? When is black white and white black and where can you claim your love so street-goers won't spit, and how did I, learning to count in Spanish for this slum dance, think I could match of all things a black-and-white swan ballet?

∽

We walk the long way back to Sammy's, along the Hudson, its waters dark and flat like they could be Swan Lake. We walk without touching, side by side, paces matched at last, and I tell Sammy the other ways the story ends.

"Russian and Chinese ballets kill off the sorcerer," I say. "That way, the swan princess becomes human and marries the prince."

"A Hollywood ending," Sammy says. "Impossibly happy."

"In one version," I say, "the swan princess kills herself. The prince jumps after her into the lake."

"That's even worse," Sammy says. "A Bollywood ending. Too melodramatic."

"In another version," I say, "the prince asks for her forgiveness.

But the swan princess dies in his arms, and the lake takes them both."

"Why should they die?" Sammy says. "They both made honest mistakes."

I don't know. I don't know anymore, between Sammy and me, me and Walt, between us three, who's the prince, the black swan, the swan princess.

Drumroll please.

"I liked tonight's ending," Sammy says. "She stays a swan, he stays a prince, and they part. Sad but real. A modern love story."

And there I have it.

THE STARS OF
BOLLYWOOD HOUSE

Raw Kordoi, Salted

2 carambola

1 teaspoon salt

1 teaspoon chaat mix

1. Wash and slice carambola into stars.
2. Season with chaat and salt to taste.
3. Mix in by hand. Enjoy.

BHUPEN

I blame that stupid boy. I could always smell a fish in a suit, even one sidling on bare bamboo legs into the restaurant. All us men paused with our knives to look. *Punjabi, Massachussetts, law,* he said in one unsure breath. I should've told her—untried hands, trembling lips—*half-cooked meat should always be sent back to the kitchen.* But she sat between us, before the drunk face of Meena Kumari, and said, "Baba, he's heard all about our Assam tea." So I slipped off to the kitchen, where the men hummed wedding tunes, and I added extra chilies to the momos, the pakoras, the pithas I laid before him. *Burn, you capitalist son of a babu,* I smiled, *if you end this badly.*

Though what good is it to rewind? If I were left with an old man, I too would weep. I too would shuffle through a Jersey studio, shrinking—130 to 98—into Bollywood movies. Every evening, I bring sour tomato-and-lime tenga all children love; New Year's pithas handrolled with sugared sesame; bitter eggplant roasted and mashed with cilantro and salt. But every evening, Jumi turns to the screen: doe-eyed Nutan wailing to the moon, tipsy Meena dancing on broken glass, the hunched shoulders of long-faced Nargis. Every midnight, she rises and roams, trailing starfruit on the concrete. The one food she touches flares in the dark.

When Jumi first left, I looped Lawrenceville two hours before finding stars that led to her theater lot. She crouched on the curb, staring at a dead deer, their tawny forms draped along the sidewalk.

Except the deer's smashed skull fell over the curb, its antlers an up-turned crown, blood unfurling from its jaw like a movie carpet.

"Ma," I said, sitting behind her, "you will get sick."

"My whole body aches," she said.

"It's not safe to walk around so late."

She snorted. "I walked around later in Jackson Heights."

"I'll make us something at home."

She grabbed at her knees. "You're not *listening*. He's gone. He didn't *like* us."

"You have to forget some things."

She whirled about as if I'd hit the deer. "When you're gone, who'll I have? In all your time at the restaurant, did you plan for that?"

It is true. Small-boned like birds, slim-numbered so even Indians ask, *Assam where*, a duo that, minus one, wouldn't be a family at all. True too: sooner or later, I will be another man down. Each night Jumi flicks on movies, I riffle through X-rays for a heart larger than even I've tried to make it. Pulpy, oval, dripping—the fruit I've eaten lodged inside. "Wear and tear will catch you," the doctor says. "Leakage will make the pressure drop." I nod but know, all fruit ripens, then bursts. When mine does, I will offer Jumi every sour piece. *You may not like this but I promise it is yours.*

Though I said nothing, just stared at the still-still maples, waiting for dawn to rustle up their flutter, the deer. When the light did spill over the asphalt, the shuddering leaves swept dust at the coming cars. The deer blazed: every ruby clotted between every hair, those glazed eyes that stayed on us. As if we were the full-grown road kill. I winged Jumi up then in my left arm, the way I had when she'd been a pigtailed girl who'd burst out leaden school doors and hidden her face in my onion-scented shirt. Except she trembled now, so hard that, for several blocks, I thought she'd seize. Only at the base of her stairs did I notice my soaked sleeve and, as I hoisted her step-by-step, I said, "Think of the past as a dream. Now you've awoken."

She jerked away—"I don't want your useless advice"—and flung off her clogs, stumbled to the cot. Several minutes later, she snored toward the wall.

From then on, I drove between the studio and the restaurant, turning onto Bronx River Parkway only for meds or mail. Our avenue would be stickered with leaves the wind had rustled off oaks and the damp stoops would be sweet with musk. The house, strewn with clothes and teacups, was a mausoleum, where all I wanted was to corpse under a comforter. Instead, I stared at my tiny outline in the hanging lamp and wondered, how could anyone wander on stars alone?

Last night, I found her sobbing before a display of wedding necklaces, which shimmered in the frosted Shop-A-Lot. I lay my hand on her braid but she pounded her fists on the sidewalk. "Get away from me!" Then she leapt up and marched across the pavement, past the Indian grocery, the Korean laundry, the shops adorned with silent brass gods. Each time she reached the L-end curb, she trekked through the lot of floating receipts and sobbed in Assamese. How she was stuck in this crummy life, how she hated being from a nothing family, how could he have said what he said after everything.

"Jumi! Listen!" I called as we hiked into wind that sliced our cheeks and tossed my cries to the ice rink fields. But round she marched and muttered, so I followed her until the night's dots petered out into a warm pink sky, cars slowed to honk, and I slumped. Knee-sore before the jewel display, I shook—Jumi turned—I wept— her pupils thinned into a cat's. Thing was, a hundred times I'd tracked her and a hundred more times I'd go, but she wouldn't answer to her name. What I'd chosen for her in the hallway where the doctor had said, "Mr. Saikia, we couldn't save your wife." Still, I'd written a good name on the clipboard and whispered a second, my mother's, into her ear for luck.

"You're cold." Jumi rested her hand on my scalp.

"I'm tired." I didn't mention the doctor's visit.

With a hoarse laugh, she hauled me up. We walked arms linked, down Oaktree Road, its flatland sides sheathed with snow and light.

Jumi spoke: the first time Walt had visited Jackson Heights, he'd suggested they play a game. They would tell the shop ladies they were marrying. They moved from spot to spot, Jumi slipping on the heaviest sets studded with rubies and emeralds, Walt assessing each nose ring, bangle, jhumka. Always, the ladies cooed over what a pretty couple they made, asked for the shaadi details.

"It's amazing how easily he lied," Jumi said. "How elaborate the stories got."

A Delhi extravaganza with painted elephants; a pier reception of Boston's finest families; a train-hopping honeymoon through Europe's museums.

"I would've held it here," she said. "I would've picked India, where he'd never been."

The streets hummed with men speeding in their sedans, with secretaries stanced on corners for buses. I wanted to say something about timing—about luck as we climbed her slippery stairs—but Jumi spoke about the theater. How long a leave she'd been given, which dancers had taken her place, who leapt in brittle bodies with the ferocity of wolves. She spoke like it was an ordinary day in these lawn-mowed parts where neighbors smile while taking one step back. Slept like it was an ordinary night, soundly, while I splashed my face, slicked down my thin side hair.

For sleep or no sleep, there is still Bollywood House. If there's one thing I know, it's that life can pink-slip you on any count: wife, country, job. Why, nights Jumi sleeps, I spread my arms to the patient moon. *Come to us,* I whisper to my memories. *Come home.*

Star One

Mostly, Jumi, I see Pita buckling on his knees. In red muck we'd furrowed, me tightroping behind him, thumbing seeds into his careful holes. The afternoon your aunts called about the heart attack, I shut myself in the freezer, between the chicken and lamb limbs. Still, Pita's eagle face flooded up, how he'd lain nose-deep in soil, too stiff to turn for air. That was precious dirt for you, sparkling jags Pita once rubbed between his forefingers. *Nothing will ever smell as sweet.* I was only sixteen then—ready to run from that mudhole—and thought, *So romantic, Pita. So wrong.*

Two days later, who but a lost son bumped in a rickshaw back into the gao? The road as unnerving as ever: green pools along its gravel edges, rippling rice khetis that, with the first rain, would suck these huts up. Women crowded every door, saris drawn across angular faces so that the blackest eyes bore holes into my back. Men turned from their tea-slurping in shops, rooster-clucking against scooters to stare, then spit. Children, as bare-and-loose-limbed as I'd been, scrambled beside the driver. *Bidekhi ahise! Bhupen Mama ahise!* As if I were a fallen god, a stranger even. I slipped into their chapped hands, the singsong of my sister's cries from the threshold, even the choppy runs of the cows and birds that flew straight at you before swerving away.

Pita lay in the drawing room, blanketed with rose-and-marigold garlands, like some official. They had dressed him in the silk shirt and dhoti he'd worn three years before, when he'd sat on the bed and rested a shaky hand on my wedding headdress. *Don't be long, Bh-*

upen. I kissed his cold toes, his swollen hands—two days dammed inside—and stroked his sunken cheeks. How could I tell him now? I would've called but the village has no phone; I would've written but you couldn't read; I would've come sooner but the restaurant ate all the money. *Too late-too late* a bulbul shrieked from the roof. Women wailed in the next room, men smoked under the tamul trees, and children peered through the window bars, giggling.

Pita, the village storyteller who'd gathered them round our courtyard fire to recite Ramayana tales, lay mute under his ruffled cover.

"He called for you," my sisters said over rice and khar, though they didn't ask why I hadn't come. Just Ba, chewing paan in the corner, said, "America must feel like heaven compared to this." It felt far, though every aerogramme that landed on our Bronx table seemed like another ticking bomb. Always, they were naming the dead. A cousin who'd pummeled drunk into another truck, a nephew snipered by a paddycat who'd once been his comrade, a niece, married to a *kaaniya* eater, who'd hung herself in the bedroom. "A man must look out for himself," I told my sisters over the phone and yet, again and again, I was yanked.

Back in Jackson Heights, I'd wheel my cart into some crowded aisle and find starfruit sitting like some far-flung relative between the mango and papaya. My heart would tremor before faces surged through me: Mai frying stars over the clay hearth, pushing salted bits at me in a silver bowl; Pita pruning kordoi branches, sun mottling him into a dark cheetah the Brits had long hunted out; my cousin cycling me atop his ramp, his basket of stars beckoning, every tangy orb the taste of those luminescent fields where we'd batted; and Tara, arm twining about her stick that first night, its top burning like the sun, all that inexplicable *Oxomiya* heat.

I couldn't imagine, four years later, I'd be laying Tara atop blazing sticks. That the stench of her meat, marrow, oil would sting my nostrils. That her brothers, lined five-strong along the Brahmaputra, would pour her dust into the rushing waters. The sun, which swells into a dripping wound there, lit every fisherman, recruit, and junkie shooting for something. As if we all burned with need. Later, crouched about a fire they'd built before a beach dhaba, her brothers passed around a black-and-white photograph of her last wedding minutes. Tara stood, a waif thronged by these tall, bearded men, under a canopy speckled with moths and lanterns. Brightest of all were their pale faces, stern Ahom brows over steepled Ahom eyes, questioning the camera. As if *America* were a bug stuck in their throats. Though her brothers learned to speak it that last evening, asking me to *leave America,* to bring you, Jumi, *home.*

I couldn't trouble them, there was no work, you were too young. What I meant was home was too exacting: asking for both eyes when you wanted to be seen, for your heart when you put forth your rice bowl. Why I rise every unexpected night, in this picture-perfect hell-freeze, tracking what's left to me. Why I'll follow stars round corners for a hundred years, rather than land before that watery snake, murmuring grace for another theft. Look at us: Ahom and Koch, we who were once kings, swatted like flies, yoked like mules. We who no longer recall ourselves. Tribal? Non-tribal? Other Backward Caste? No one in America makes heads or tails of this junk, so long as your wallet speaks. But home will spear you to the ground, so that you're another Cat-Eye left to rot.

But the clearest reason, Jumi, is because you were born all me: sun-dark skin, fire-engine fury. Why I snapped a hundred pictures of you, mailed them to the village, wrote in Assamese: *our blood.* Even then, we knew: only ragged faces and half-stories left to trade over fire, and the ULFA blackouts, the state machinery had dimmed those too. Why, when you screamed, a baby unchoked by Tara's blood, I'd phoned the men.

"She lives! In America!"

"Tara?" they said.

And though the old name sanded into my gut, I wrote the new one on the hospital paper.

"Prarthana," I said. "Prayer."

Boiled Kordoi, Mashed

3 carambola
1 saucepan hot water
1 tablespoon mustard oil
1 teaspoon salt

1. Heat water to a boil.
2. Add unskinned carambola. Leave until gold color turns green and skin may be peeled with fingernail.
3. Drain and rinse carambola in cold water, then dry with napkin.
4. Mash with spoon or hand to pulp.
5. Add oil and salt. Should be spicy but easy to swallow.

Bhupen

This afternoon, she begins early, locking herself in the bathroom, banging her head against the bathtub rim.

When I ask her to let me in, to just try me, she says, "Stop acting like you know! You didn't grow up here. You never even dated."

My hand slips off the knob. "Maybe you're right. I don't know a lot of things. But your uncles think you're beautiful. You are a star in my heart."

She sobs low to the ground, more fiercely, waves broken by hiccups. Several minutes later, I kneel and say, "Ma, please open."

Her cries trickle to sniffles and she says, "I don't want anyone to see me."

"Seeing you like this," I say, "is not good for me either."

The door opens to her bowed head, hair tufting up like a nest. I kiss her forehead and her hot arms circle my waist.

"Let's go to the restaurant," I say. "Make a list of things you want."

She names simple things—movies, bangles, chaat—that bring us back. To streets and streets bustling with skinny boys in button-down shirts, with grizzled sardars passing *Blowout!* fliers before bhangra-thumping shops, with high-cheeked Nepalis cabbing narrow passes, with curl-tongued Southies ladling up dosas and uttapam, with women . . . so many women! . . . in chiffon saris and sequined salwars, jhumkas twitching from earlobes, diamonds glittering on beaks, whispering of this one's no-good husband, that one's American-style son, with munchkins whose black eyes and lush hair shine over stained tees while blowing bubbles at stalled cars, with hip-haired gazelles loping arm-in-arm past jittery-eyed cubs loitering by hydrants, past old-timers in kaftans brooding over plaques of Mecca and pot-bellied Bengali script, past hole-in-the-walls curtained and placarded *Patel Grocery, Raj Sweets, Singh Electronics*, past the brick rises and the postered theater and the dingy subway stairs teeming with beige-and-gold waves of like-and-unlike faces. To the splattered concrete corner of Thirty-Seventh and Roosevelt. Between the saffron walls, the Christmas lights, the bamboo innards of Bollywood House.

The men are crowded round the carom board when Jumi and I step into the dim hall. *Arein!* they cry and buzz toward her, swarming us under the tasseled thangka. Like the day I brought Jumi in my stiff arms, a mewling bundle they passed around with comic coos till she smiled. "Jumi," they say, "why you don't come no more?" Except they step back now at her shorn hair, loose hoodie, baggy cords that make her seem a twelve-year-old dressed in men's things. She stares back—at our cratered eyes, cheekbones jutting from oil-splotched skin—and says, "I work now too." No one asks if she dances still. Only Latha echoes from the radio in the closet and Jumi, as if directed, walks to the carom board and traces a line through the boric powder. "Can I play?"

For an hour, in the shadow of a Ganesh murti, under the halo of flickering lamps, it's us five again. Dorji and Jumi stacking the black, white, and red chips into a *kolgos* column, the boys waving me over and clanging spoons, sizzling up pots in the kitchen. "Bhupen," they say, "worrying so much won't help. You must tell her what we know about love."

We practice first, Dorji *thwacking!* the yellow striker so the tree of chips topples and *ping!* a ten-point blue zooms into a corner hole. "I'm back!" he says, rubbing his palms as if to spark fire. Jumi stays a zombie beside his gleeful cackles, his rising chips, so Vikas sits beside her and pours her a cup. "Can't let the old ones win, yeah? Watch how you do it."

Chips realigned into a many-pointed star, the game begins.

Vikas's Cheshire smile spreads over his chocolate planes—that face that launches a hundred women's cravings—before he *whfft! whfft!* bags two white pieces. *Like the pasty girls you've been juggling since you left your greencard wife,* I want to say. I never liked Beatrice, a blimp with an angry face drawn on, but never disliked her either, especially when she advised Jumi about boys.

"Fluke," Dorji says, but Vikas furrows his brows over the fifty-point queen. He flicks his middle finger and *pfft!* the striker slides into the hole instead, so that he has to slam a white piece back onto the board.

"He gambles like this too," Imran tells Jumi. "That's why he still works here."

The men laugh, tapping their chips on the board's thick sides. Vikas slaps Imran's head and says, "At least I have an excuse. What's yours?"

Imran taps one forefinger on his long Persian nose and perches the other over the striker, setting up an impossible diagonal cut at the red queen. "Jumi, I met Aisha when I was younger than you. She worked at her father's store. Always talking about how they made this chair, that table. Always wearing these funny glasses." He loops his fingers round his eyes in o's. "She was going to start her own furniture business when she got out of school." He flicks the striker—a quick line—it barely misses the queen.

"Did she?" Jumi says, the first question outside herself in months.

"This striker is no good," he says. "Her last letter, they moved her home from the hospital. Once she's better, she'll start looking."

For what? More immigration dreams that will never happen, not for a Muslim girl with HIV? The last letter had a photo: Aisha skinny as an Indian cow, ribs showing under her sari, eyes like a fortune-teller's globe.

Dorji slides the striker left-right along the striking alley, as if aiming for the cheap blues clustered there. One eye shut, *fft!* he sends the queen *plop!* into the farthest hole.

"Security! Security!" the men roar. Dorji sideswipes a blue into the closest hole and fox-grins at Jumi. "See if they can beat that!" The blood up in his scarred fingers, he straight-hits blues into hole after hole. Aiming for the fourth blue, he says, "Jumi, I am only half a man. You know why?"

Her lips twitch. "Because you're short?"

"Because half of me is in Nepal with my son. Every time I phone my wife there, she says, 'He asks about you. When are you coming back?' Then my wife here says, 'Your body is here but your heart is there.'"

"You married Moni?" Jumi says, meaning the shapely sphinx who waits in the hall every midnight closing.

Dorji pauses, scouting for a white. "What could I do? When I was there and Moni told me she was going to America, I thought I would die."

We freeze, only Dorji not hearing his own import, until a white piece thuds off—up!—over the side.

Vikas grabs the striker away. "Don't be greedy, sahib."

"Finish the board," I say and start stacking the teacups. In fifteen minutes, the other servers will rush in with stained shirts, customers will tinkle open the door, the restaurant will heat up with nerves and supper stories. But with only three whites left, Vikas positions the striker to ricochet a nearby white, and says, "Maybe in India, it's find a wife, settle down, have kids. But here?" He bangs two into the hole and assuredly sets up another ricochet, a slimmer-angled one. "There's a million girls waiting to give it up. White, black, Spanish. American girls," he pauses to point at Jumi, "are the problem for girls like you."

Jumi hunches, slipping back into her smashed shell.

"Enough," I say, clamping my hand over the last piece, so the striker rams off my pinky. "Go clean up."

Vikas throws up his hands but Imran yanks him up, shoves him toward the back tables. "You would've lost anyway."

An hour in, as Vikas and Imran hustle the floor, as Dorji and I sizzle up kebabs, curries, momos in the back wing, Jumi stands like an apparition by the door. She holds menus to her heart as if she can't bear handing them over, glares at hand-holding couples as if she'd rather shoot than serve them. Vikas and Imran push her now and then to some fork-waving customer, some beer-drunk Punjabi, but she cannot pour the lassi without splotching the tablemats, cannot stop her tie from falling into soups. The customers blink and cut the tip—but who hasn't seen boys shuffling in, shoveling up a two-person course while skimming a book? Or mummy-wrapped girls shuffling in before the Friday rush, to pick at a samosa and sip cheap wine? Who hasn't tasted lovesickness in the darkest corner of their own house?

That's what I ask myself tonight when I find Jumi not outside but in the bathroom again, sprawled in vomit. The starfruit I bought and sliced today are dumped in the bathroom bin. The vomit pool is pulpy green-gold, like the rotten fruit I'd dredged up in my net from the home pond. She stirs on an elbow, moaning, as I press her wrists for her pulse.

"We shouldn't have given you all that food," I say as I lift her torso. "Your system still can't tolerate it."

Her teeth chatter, her limbs quiver as I lift her to stand. "What's the point, Baba? Just leave me here."

"How can you be so dramatic?" I drag her to the cot, tuck blankets about her, and cannot tell if the quaking of the fuzzy fabric is her back or mine. "Have you thought about me? You are all that keeps me here!"

She rolls away to the wall, weeping in such muffled bursts that I barely make out her words. How he's moved on, how he prefers white girls to her, how everyone said he was too good for trash like her. "Am I trash?" she says. "Am I never gonna be good enough?"

"How can you listen to him?" I say, though I am well-acquainted with the verse. How many times had the village kids said, "Bhupen, you won't get out"; the college boys said, "Look at the midget hick"; the Indians said, "I smell a fish-eating tribal"; the Americans said, "Go back to where you came from, Injun." So I smooth her hair, wipe her moist face. "If I listened to people, we wouldn't be here."

"What did we gain?" she says, turning to me, her eyes narrowed and cheeks flushed. "I saw what's happened there. No one wants us to make it anywhere."

A fact for which I have counters, but who will tip a glass to moisten my lips as I do to hers, who will slide a thermometer along my cheek as I do along hers? It reads a number her weight should be—104 while the morning scale pointed to 97—and when I rummage through the latest journal to record this, I find other numbers I've begun tracking. Numbers that have started to run past Jumi's column, double digits clogging my vessels, triple beats throbbing against my veins. It's then, my pen poised to add Jumi's number on the left that I remember my stress test for this coming morning. "The necessary next step," the doctors had said, but how can I leave my child now?

I call the women: wives of engineers I'd once known, before I'd fallen through the cracks with a baby. "Ki hoise?" the first one says over the phone, just as dawn breaks through the window, lighting Jumi's form on fire.

STAR TWO

Jumi, I found your mother on the street, both of us brandishing burning sticks and shouting. *Oxom dekhor oxomiya bhakha!* I marched with the Science boys, Tara with the History girls, but even across the street, she seemed an unearthly crane. Wispy mane, kohled eyes, creamy skin, why I watched her as we tramped over Guwahati's red gutters, through its marigold mazes, along the river that swelled as if it would join us. I must have seemed a monkey beside her stick, which looked hand-carved by some servant. I'd filched mine from Pita's grove. He hadn't wanted me to *meet the state* but he'd taught us boys too well. A hundred afternoons, we'd climbed his trees thick with green-gold fruit, swung from branch to branch, before perching on the highest, the lithest. Up there, mooning over the purple buffalo treading veins into the mossy earth, we'd plucked as many stars as we wished. We'd salted their crunchy points. We'd feasted like kings.

Until we spotted white men circling our fields in helicopters. They lay, along the village road, a pipe that pulled oil from Assam and funneled it to Bihar. At first, people whispered of smooth roads that would take us straight to Delhi, of jobs that would house and school us all. But the elders had seen Nehru leave us to the Chinese and shook their heads. In the end, their bitter words were all we got. Every morning, every afternoon, we walked by that steel snake on our way to class and listened to our own dark gold rushing by us. Evenings, we lingered in cotton jumpers by the main road as older students trampled the rock-strewn roads. *Tel xarodaghar amak lagibo!* The flames they held up merged into a seething beast and we sensed, as it wound toward the dust fuming from the plains, we were headed the same way.

No wonder, Jumi, I spoke to your mother in a cell. We were crammed in, hundreds of students, into damp cubes stinking of pee and sweat. A single window, dim as a star by the blood-splotched ceiling, cast our bulks into sweltering shadows, our voices into breathy cursing. At our luck, the cops who were our own, the Brits who'd noosed Bengali on us. Kismet or qayamat—you tell me, Jumi—but Tara's back happened to press mine. "You sound," she said, "like a broken harmonium." I hadn't realized I was humming— the quick beats of *Junglee*, how I didn't care if anyone thought I was wild—but when she sang, a wistful, raspy alto, I had to turn. Her spine vibrated like a snake's, the cell swelled with music as shadow after shadow sang with her: lokogeets, borgeets, Bollywood tunes. So that up-close, in the spray of light, she was even more startling: the high bones of our people, that ancient woolly hair, those delicate limbs crossed over her cotton sari.

I would've spoken, Jumi, but I forgot words outside the chorus. We'd all forgotten: that we didn't know what the cops would do in the morning, that most of our parents couldn't buy our way out, that students had been beaten for demanding Assamese in our schools, that we were thirsty because we wouldn't say the Bengali word *jol*. Song to song, we glided, reeling a new phrase off the closing one, as if we were kids playing Antakshari. *Ey!* The guards banged batons on the bars but what could they accuse us of? Their own scuff-holed shoes tapped along.

I didn't touch Tara again till the biya, when I unwrapped her gold-silk-shyness, then stood gaping. I hadn't imagined the crane would land on my bed, press its palms to my chest, say "Your heart's beating so fast." I didn't realize I was happy for happiness is a dream, as is grief. She withered when we moved here. From the river and Oxomiya of Guwahati to the snow and Spanish of the Bronx. Believe me, I'd tried to design a life, taken one hydraulics gig after another, roamed from Guwahati to Shillong to Dibrugarh to Tawang. But no one would keep an honest man, and a poor man cannot keep a wife. So we came back, Jumi, and it was in this time that I built Bollywood House, that your mother locked herself in the apartment, watching Bollywood movies. Always some plodding thing in which lovers marry or die because of money or history. She came, after all, from theatrical folk, who had ridden in from Burma on elephants, enacted our lore in courtyards with cock-and-bull sparring. Yet she'd rouse me at night, not to talk Bollywood House or re-watch movies, but to curl into my chest. Weeping *"Ghuri jao, Bhupen, please."* "What's left for us?" I'd ask. "At least," she'd say, "the past comes calling."

I heard her only months later, when she fell silent on a hospital bed, her legs spread and bloody. One minute, she'd been moaning a new mother's aches; the next, not even breathing. Just the widening star between her thighs, the baby slipping out like a squalling lamb. Then the clutter and clang of green folks, who pumped and pronged Tara, who scurried from room to monitor to computer screen, so that I barely saw her disappearing. The whole time, Jumi, you screamed from a stranger's arms.

So you see, what I know about love is this: the heart stops in many ways, often without reason. Blood stains without warning—soil, ceiling, hospital gown. From your own fruit gutted and smashed on you by a heckling universe, doomed poison bursting from within.

Kordoi Tarkari

5 carambola
1 green chili
1 tablespoon mustard seeds
1 teaspoon turmeric
2 tablespoons oil
   salt

1. Chop carambola into strips. Mince green chili.
2. Mix gold and green chop and coat with turmeric.
3. In a vat, heat oil and fry mustard seeds until they pop.
4. Add carambola strips and chili. Be sure mustard seeds
   are spread throughout.
5. Add salt to taste. Serve hot.

BHUPEN

One by one, this over-sunny morning, the women come. Perching on the edge of Jumi's cot, twisting a rag in water, mopping her warm face. And gazing at this hideout of brass jars filled with spears, fraying tapestries of Buddhas, toppled Bollywood DVDs. But ladies that they are, they munch on nimkis and ask the usuals about Bollywood House. After my switch with Dorji, I'd fallen into a crevice from which I'd spy their parties. Which lady wore the most trussed-up mekhla, whose daughter had turned to drink, whose son had landed which Wall Street job. My own news—my own heart—they will spill to their men while folding silk pajamas, oiling their husbands' backs. *Saikiar obosta,* they'll say in hushed tones that mean, *don't let this happen to us.*

Pinkie Ba, the oldest of the ladies, drives over late afternoon. She marches up the steps with her bulldog face, square tribal bones set in a villager's solid build, a Corning dish of chicken soup in her hands. Like a Kamrupi, she peers right into my face. "Who was the lora?" I walk to the living room window, its deluge of white light and empty cars, as I mumble his parting words, and she shakes her head. "How do their brains work? Must be what these Americans say. Money doesn't buy manners." I turn to Ba and, fists trembling, want to confess: I've dreamt of snapping every bone in his buttered body, stewing his entrails in a curry I'd serve his fancy friends. But it is Ba who turns away, kneeling in her bulky pink sweater by the DVDs strewn before the TV. "You look like a ghost, Bhupen. Go take a walk."

I almost ask if she can stay the night. So I can muster the put-off drive for my EKG? So I can slow into this thing called sleep? But I kneel to alphabetize the familiar faces—Meena, Nutan, Vyjantima-la—and say, "Baidew? What will I do if something happens?"

Ba brushes away my hand. "With manu coming in and out? You worry too much. Jowa."

So I make a list of things—egg, bread, xaak—I will eat if Jumi won't, and scarf my head into the iced streets. Oaktree Road mills with families, about sari shops, dosa joints, the fragrant grocery. I wheel my cart among them—straight-backed Punjabis, lotus-eyed Southies, the ceaseless chirp of Bengalis—and hear the oddest heartbeats. *Gagone. Ta-rara. Ju-mima.* I wheel about with the cart, its stiff wheel squeaking, the sole man *one-one-one*, listening-looking at this small aisle on this small road where I've landed. Plain green gourds that, hacked, would stink with orange sweetmeat. Fuzzy fingers that, boiled, would melt into peppered okra soup. I wheel up and down aisle one—selecting samosas, a coriander bunch, tamarind pods—along frayed linoleum aisles Tara never visited. Her perimeter had been our Castle Hill Avenue block, which she circled endlessly before collapsing on the sofa before re-watching a Bollywood film.

Too late, too late, the bulbul sings. Everywhere, contented men shift beside careful women, so I turn into the jewelry aisle. But here, it is all mothers and daughters, a skinny salesgirl clucking about them like a hyper chicken. *Oh but this blue suits her skin; oh but gold is good luck; oh but you can't have too many bangles.* No one glances at me, a short man in a loose coat, loafers scruffed up. No one bothers to ask, *sir, for whom are you shopping?* No one circles-and-checks as I finger this set of pink glass bangles, that row of long brass jhumkas, or drop extra goodies into an extra bag. Hadn't Jumi wept before such trinkets? Hadn't Walt played with them and her? No one notices as I lift my trinket bag alone, leaving the vege-tables in the bangle bin. Even I don't quite notice as I wander to the exit with my trinkets . . . *beep-beep* . . . mothers and daughters, men and wives turn to me with their questioning frowns. *Beep-beep. Not for you!* And I freeze, breath caught between the fake jewels in my plastic purse and the electrodes jammed inside my leaky heart. And the women smoke about me in a chattering, hand-wringing haze. And I sink, trinkets cascading out in a rainbow on the tiled floor. And I lie atop the gray linoleum crinkling up into tiny hills, arms knotted, legs jerking. Till only dark lips and ringed claws peck at my cheeks, my chest sinking beneath the snow: ospreys and larks and chickadees. But where oh where is my tongue?

Atop a mound of slippery fat, blackening peel, marrow-red bone, I hold my daughter. Twelve still, just before she'd slink off into a mumbling adolescence I couldn't translate, she flutters her eyes wide and grabs my chin. "You have to speak! Say something, other than we're not good enough!" But the vinegar of the mound, of the moaning around us, from mummies lashed to branches with rope, rushes into my nostrils, my throat. And when I grunt up on my elbows, my knees—to point and say, *we're so close, ma*—Jumi rolls away as if in a playground game—*pffishhwhoo*—bumpily down the mound. I dive in, swimming deep through the thicket of other people's fruit rinds and crumbling crusts, till—*dhum!*

I wake on a stretcher in the back of a van, two boys pressing this glass tourniquet and pumping that rubber dial over my tingling arms, my fast chest. And it is not Jumi but Dorji at my feet, stubble shadowing his slow smile.

"How're you feeling, Mr. S?" the darker boy says, his hands deftly checking the circles pasted just under my collarbone.

Pani is all I can breathe out but who understands here?

"Arein," Dorji says, slipping a plastic cup of water to my mouth. "What is this fainting drama in public? You too are forgetting to eat now?"

"I was shopping," I say but, voice whistling, it comes more like *I was stopping.*

"Do you have arrhythmia?" the bulkier boy says, rolling up his sleeves to forearms tattooed with faces, pressing two fingers to my neck, my wrists, the sore between my ribs. "Your friend here connected us with your doctor who said you were due for an EKG." He steps back, eyebrows raised and stethoscope paused in his left hand, as if expecting an apology.

Dorji pats my hands and shakes his head. "It's a family syndrome, this fasting protest. His daughter is also stubborn."

The thinner boy raises me up slowly to a sit-up on the stretcher. "You're better to her alive than dead. Am I right, Mr. S?"

They slip then, these strapping kids with smooth faces closeting their own reels, into snappy Spanish as they riffle through yellow pages on clipboards. Dorji laces my loafers and says, "yaar, we aren't immortal anymore. We've become . . . what they call it here? Endangered species?"

Which makes no sense, I want to scold him as he signs yellow papers and thanks the boys, who watch curiously as Dorji lifts my left leg, then my right over the back rim of the van.

It is all I can do to stand swaying against the brisk rush of wind. To hobble after Dorji between the van and his Corolla as he zooms. To breathe *one-in-two-out* over the hilly highway, past the jagged smoke stacks, the cluster of pink houses, round the forested side lane that opens up to manicured lawns.

Except the lurid lights of a cop car swirl in Jumi's lot, by the corner of pink begonias, the snow-spotted sign "Peace Terrace." Pinkie Ba, whose pink sweater is gone yet dabs at sweat from the sides of her neck, turns from the two cops standing wide-stanced before their car. "Bhupen?" she says, spinning, then waggles and arm-pumps to Dorji and me.

"I called you so many times!"

"Where is she?" I say.

Ba blinks rapidly and looks not at me but behind to Dorji. "Bhupen, my daughter called," she says rapidly. "The babysitter had cancelled, I was gone for just a moment . . . ."

I don't wait for an ending—I skip-step after Dorji—to the rumpled mound of sheets. Kordoi uncut and untouched on the plate, so that there are no clues. Not one.

Star Three

Jumi, we'd gather kordoi from the jungle, wrenching their pliant bodies from wild soil, matting their trunks upon our backs, whistling lokogeets all the way to our crosshatched gates. Hole by hole, we dug with our hands, we lined their bodies and foretold, farm kids, our losses: which would not outlast the rains, which would not unfurl past a few years. Still, we squatted, stuffing cauliflower, eggplant, cabbage about crunchy roots. When we sat back, slim trunks rose before us, sentinels ready to drop their luscious grenades.

Nothing like the soldiers who camped near downtown, for this ULFA skirmish or that tribal gondogol, dark Indians who scanned us with radar eyes over hawk noses. As if we were the aliens. Sometimes, when they tired of the store dal-bhat, they rapped on our doors, and Mai would simmer maas-mangxo over the fire, would grumble how we had barely enough for eight. But the soldiers, lounging on bamboo muras on the porch, simply watched us kids scamper round the courtyard, chant in a tag game. *Kabaddi-kabadi-kabadi!* They watched us as if they themselves might knock us, rifles perched on their knees, fingers tweedling in pockets over the sweetest girls. Girls whom Ma wouldn't name but who neighbors reported as loigoise. *Taken.* Though by whom and for what, no one said. I pieced together the shards, saw ourselves refracted stretched-out ways. I saw the twelve-year-old skinnies who slunk in corners, went straight from house to well to outhouse, nowhere beyond. I saw the newspapers spread on teachers' desks, brown bodies laid out across the front page, faces bagged so you couldn't name whose son it had been, whose brother you had jostled with, which uncle you had followed on a hunt, a swim.

Once, while netting fish, I'd even seen a Bodo boy from the next village. He'd left a year before—NDFB, folks said—the way so many Dadas had, slipping out kitchen doors. Slipping back in with money, a uniform, a claim. I was wading in with a net when my feet bumped a seeming log that had drifted up. He must've been carried underwater for several days, his limbs puffed and bluish, his face a fraying mask. Half his right jaw had been scooped away, either by the teeth of an animal, a stone, or a man's knife. I knelt in the water, so no tiger or soldier would think I was prey, and touched the stringy tendons of his cheek, the plush ridges of his hacked tongue. The cut was too clean for an accident or animal, so that, as I stroked the even leather of that pink hill, I wondered: *what had he said to warrant this? Where had the cut end gone?* Maybe it had melted into the river that, yearly, nearly drowned us all; or crumbled into this dense soil, to be sucked up by some sapling, transfigured into a kordoi I'd slice off for my own eager tongue.

I stepped forward to turn him upright, drag him up, but stumbled on loose pebbles—*splash!*—we sank under together. I gulped, half-startled, half-choking from the marsh muck and water that swelled over us. The boy's body fell heavily on me, rolling us down, down into the dank pit of the lake, his arms and legs tangled with mine, his face blooming *whoosh* like the lake-bottom plants. It was a scape of pink muscle and white bone and gelatin eye, the torn fibers waving toward me, the sides bursting open to blank lenses that mirrored my own dark, pocked, strained face. His jaw dropped fully from the fragile strings, as if about to snap, float away, leaving only that shredded tongue that licked at my nose, my eyes. As if he were kissing me to swim and stay in his gentle embrace, the river's rocking, that private, salty moment. I'd known such a lull as a fishing kid, plunging into cold water, into morose green depth, air rich in my lungs, floating free of all land things. How, for a few moments, you wonder if you could live down here, leaving men to dream among the darting fish. But then plain human need daggers your lungs and you wriggle up for breath. Like that, with his tongue wooing mine, his hug brothering me, my brain pounded-pulsed. And I shoved his face, so that it cracked in a sharp left drop onto his shoulders, and kicked his knees in so that I shot—*out! up!*—to the gauzy light.

Jumi, I know what lurks underneath. What you too maybe found, your year dancing on those banks, the dead I never named. How you must have sunk, when you returned to a boy who would not embrace you. Who said you were too Indian when you didn't feel Indian enough. Who said the most beautiful thing about you was your undertow, your giving in. Who said your dark, unsure look was too much like his. Full of bloody currents, scooped out cheek, a tongue-ing lost somewhere loamy—unsavory clues others might call garbage but that I patiently read.

Kordoi Tenga

5 unripe carambola

1 lime

1 dried red chili

1 tablespoon mustard seeds

1 teaspoon flour and 1 cup water

1 teaspoon sugar

1 teaspoon salt

2 tablespoons oil

1. Heat oil and mustard seeds in vat till they sound.
2. Choose green carambola for sourness. Chop into cubes and add to vat.
3. Break up chili by hand and add shreds to vat.
4. Stir-fry mix for several minutes on medium heat until carambola chop tenderizes.
5. Add flour and water mix to vat. Cook for several more minutes to light boil.
6. Add lime juice, sugar, and salt, and lower heat. Cook for last several minutes, adding any of the last three ingredients for desired blend of sweet and sour taste, though sour should dominate.

BHUPEN

Useless police. They swirl their lights, poke about Jumi's studio, misspell *Partana* for *Prarthana, 100 lbs.* for *80.* A no-neck cop lingers last, yanking open drawers of knives, the fridge putrid with foiled food, while Dorji brews a saucepan of tea. A slow rite: pouring water and milk in equal inches, heating the liquid to foam, grating in ginger, sifting in sugar, plopping cinnamon sticks last. A caramel disc, the tea fumes from a cup I cradle as No-Neck thuds about the bathroom, bangs the toilet seat, rattles the curtain rings, and says, "The paint's worn off the sink."

"Stomach acid," I say. "She isn't good at cleaning."

No-Neck stalks to our table and rubs his throat, as if it were he who had thrown up.

Dorji lifts a cup. "Would you like some?"

No-Neck gazes out the window, at daffodils crystallized in frost. "It's a hard job."

"She couldn't have gone far, no?" Dorji says.

"It's a hard job," No-Neck says, patting wisps across his pate. "Being a father."

We sip a cup to the fridge hum, and No-Neck promises his partner in the morning. When his blue-striped car growls round the corner onto the freeway, Dorji rests his hand on my knee. "You tell me where we should go."

It's like the old days, when Dorji and I would drive our latest wheels through blurred city lanes. We'd roll down the glass and lean our faces out to catch the salty rush. Now Dorji steers his Corolla along spotless roads and we tighten our windows against the chill. Bank after mall, grass without geese, houses even and pink. *Must feel like heaven*, Ba had said, but the town feels locked. In dimmed houses, engineers and doctors I once knew sleep beside fat, fussy wives. Tara would have stayed slim, would have braided her cloud, would have known where a sad woman goes.

Dorji steers—I squint—circling, circling.

Dorji mutters about Americanized kids as he turns into a gleaming black lot of cafés and clothing stores, an IMAX theater at its far end by the shrub row. How many times had I found Jumi sitting under the blazing red letters of the latest titles? Dorji pauses before the glass doors and it is ourselves we see: sharp-boned faces floating between posters of golden-haired ladies in red dresses, Rambo types shouldering guns, impossible sands of blue-and-white resorts.

Dorji shakes his head. "Jumi shouldn't have come here. *We* wouldn't be here."

"So many times," I say, "she said the same thing about us."

Dorji loops away to Oaktree, blaring up the AM weather report. "Clear skies," the voice repeats, "a mild forecast." But once we step into the blackwashed lot, the silence rushes back on us, the night having erased the clang of Indians. Us crazy Indians with our crazy gods and our crazy prophecies of our crazy, fatter futures.

"She couldn't have gotten this far," Dorji says.

"She's not a little girl anymore."

"We must map the points she visited most. We must be systematic."

"You know as well as I do, systems fail. It is people who are not supposed to fail."

"Bhupen, you were always a better engineer than me. A better man. At least you are here."

"A widower with no answers?"

Dorji bows his head and marches past the shuttered fronts of stores. He limps these days, favoring his right leg, after a kitchen explosion five years ago. The vindaloo had burnt the skin all the way up his thigh, and he'd reeked of vinegar and metal for weeks. *Go home,* I'd said, wanting to protect him from customers' stares, but he'd just grimaced and marched on with that right leg.

At the fourth walk-around, Dorji puts one hand over his chest, another over mine, and spits a line of phlegm. "Tonight is a lost cause. We need to rest."

I push his hands off. "We will look when there is light. Meanwhile, we will make that map."

Dorji and the radio are mute back to Jumi's lot, where he dawdles, checking under his hood, avoiding my moist eyes and chapped face, so I plod away and up to Jumi's studio. Lights off—to her unmade bed, uneaten kordoi, DVDs scattered before the TV—titles I can recite from memory. I sit on her cot and hold my head the way I had when I'd first come home without Tara. We had rented the second floor of a Guyanese home and I'd lain on the bed, listening to Jumi wail from the crib. All night, I didn't move, until the Guyanese grandmother knocked on the door, offered her used teat to the frantic mouth, sat by me with sweetened milk in a glass. Only then, as now, could I un-hunch my chest into long, throaty breaths.

That first year, I left Jumi with the other wives, their faces like calm ponds. But then, as Jumi grew enough to crawl about the restaurants, the women faded back to their ranches of rose-and-spruce. I recorded her then—long feet, wild hair, a tot's stumble through the new Bronx house—as if Tara might show up at that door, with her square jaw set and thrumming fingers on the knob, and ask, *What scenes did I miss?* She had loved the Indian serials, camera lingering on each face, music rising through the scene, cutoff just before the resolution. She would have plopped down at the kitchen table, popped pani puri into her mouth, and asked between munches, *What does Jumi want? Who is her foe? Are you helping her fight?* Back then, I would've had a number for everything: *She is twelve and reads one fantasy book a week. She is fourteen and com-*

plains about boys who say she's too skinny. She's seventeen and has chopped off your beautiful hair. Maybe Tara would have slapped her hand on the table and laughed; maybe she would have shoved aside the plate and jabbed her finger in my forehead. *Can't you imagine, silly man, where your own child would hide?*

But in the gloom of her room, my breath fogs the outline of empty chairs, of uncut fruit, of dead Bollywood queens.

Just as I pull off my socks, Dorji bounds up the stairs. He clutches the railing, gasping, "car . . . outside . . . sleep . . . ." And I bolt, knowing and not knowing, slipping down the carpeted steps, half-scurrying-slipping across the parking lot. There is the blue Corolla again—there is the garbage bin—there, there, inside, Jumi. I press my palms to the rear window. She sleeps curled in the backseat, fists rammed into cheeks.

Dorji fiddles a key into the driver's door, and the blast of air shivers Jumi awake. I grab her bare feet, her tight shoulders, while Dorji tucks a blanket about her. Like this, we carry her—shuffle-crunch over the the thinly iced walkway—through the rosy chill of dawn. Up the stairs to the cot, where we rub-squeeze—Dorji left side, me right—her toes, palms, limbs. Jumi, Jumi—like the light creeping into every corner of her studio—loosens, breathes.

Press, rub, count—Dorji runs hot water in the bath—and I am a young father, Jumi a baby. Except Dorji had not said then, "I'll pack her things," had not carried a duffel bag of clothes down to a car, had not left me cradling this languid body into a bathtub half-filled with soapwater. Jumi sinks like a sack, only her face above the suds—a copper replica of faces I have seen a hundred times: Pita's, Tara's, the Bodo boy's, every girl corner-slinking, every boy crouching in the bush. Jumi's face twitches, lips moving with words so hoarse I can barely hear, much less speak back.

But when have I known the right words? Even when Jumi was a little frog, it was Ba who instructed me. "Support the neck, sponge the bum, don't turn away your eyes." Even when I'd done it right, my tot rose and splashed down in her seater, then giggled, and I wouldn't know whether to scold or smile. I'd simply wiped the suds from her lips—those days when I had to stop her from eating everything.

Water laps now her hollowed frame, and as I sponge this strange land, I think, *This is not a father's job.* But life never asked, *Bhupen, would you like to be top engineer or top chef? Bhupen, can you carry three half-hearts instead of a whole?* So I ask Dorji, as I towel Jumi down, slip her into jeans, pull a kurta over her head. "Can you close shop? Can you call the others? Can you drive us home?"

Star Four

Jumi, we raised this place from the dead, plank by plank, right after the laundry burned down. The streets were still *are you Catholic or Jew,* but Indians were washing up all over the city, carrying stone-hard suitcases, debating dollars versus rupees, dreaming of dove-skinned women in houses far from the stink of oil and curry. Soon as I found Dorji, I knew he was hungry: slitted coals for eyes, stocky mountain legs on which he strode round and round the luggage belt. Both of us had landed engineers' offices forever below the bosses, some Tom-Dick-or-Harry always slapping our backs. "You boys can really crunch numbers." "You people are just too polite." "You really need to speak up." "Boob." "Door."

"The name is," we'd begin, but we heard what they meant, through the memos, the Colgate smiles, the promotions that never came. *Asian Invasion Alert! Hang back, Hindoo. Keep kowtowing, coolie.*

Four years before we could pool the money, before we had the nerve to tell the boys who'd schooled with us. "Beta," they shook their heads, "a bird in the hand is all you can expect." Our mothers wept over the phone. "Did we suffer so much to die without grandchildren?" But months of munching curry chicken alone in the cafeteria while the others chomped burgers and bragged about banging Molly-Lucy-Jen, and Dorji and I were itching for a sign. So when we heard fire had ashed Jackson Heights, had turned its sky vermilion-red, we stamped our cigarettes and went.

You can't imagine how it was: an L-shaped plot covered with

what seemed the burnt-up bits of another man's dream. Night after night, over chai and biryani, we sketched and crossed out and counted, till a house of cards teetered up. Then we hammered up walls, we twisted in the pipes, we wired lights to blaze out the place, we stapled down plush carpet to go under wood chairs with fat cushions, wood tables with slender legs, we nailed to the ceiling loom weavings by Bodo girls, Naga, Mising, and over all the walls, we hung our cloth-wrapped things: purple-and-red thangkas, figurines of the gods, japis like large starred flowers, and the bamboo tools used by men who'd climbed Dorji's mountains, who'd fished Pita's lake. And along each wall, we hung the Bollywood women. Why the customers called us not by the black-and-white sign, *Himalayan Bistro*, but *Bollywood House*.

On the back left wall, by the bathroom: Meena Kumari. That sad moon face so subtle, so drunk. Dancing as the abandoned whore of *Pakeezah*, on shattered glass.

On the middle left, by the brass elephants: Madhubala. Ringlets around her hopelessly hopeful face. Dancing as Anarkali, the courtesan who, for stealing the heart of the prince, was buried alive.

On the front left, by the register: the folded crane limbs of Nutan. Singing to the moon that has come but why not her love? Sweet, sweet Nutan of *Milan*, who taught her servant lover to read.

On the back right wall, by the kitchen: Smita Patil. Slinky in that white sari in that rain, moving shyly with Amitabh. Smita who too left a baby at thirty.

On the middle right wall, by the biggest japi: Madhuri. Dancing in disguise, always barefoot, always lush, among jolly thugs. In fields or temples or bars, her bosom pulsing with pleasure.

In that front right wall, by the darkest corner: the happily twisted faces of Sridevi. Parodying fast-talking Southies, cold-shouldered Northies, the bubble-thin dreams of round-eyed girls. Sridevi, so alive with her serpent rage, her wicked grin that knows too much.

Then in the lobby: Tara. No script for the steppes of that face, her nose soft on my palm, eyes tipped like her mother's and yours. Just this photo garlanded with dried roses, set over a glass bowl of anise, smoked every morning by rosewood incense. A stranger had taken that photo, when Tara and I had climbed halfway up the dim stairwell to Lady Liberty's navel. We'd paused panting, and I'd said, "I too will feed the masses." She laughed, "We can't even make it halfway up." Some American, crossing us, stretched a hand. "Would you like a snap of the pretty lady inside the pretty lady?"

There is no space, Jumi, for another picture. Unless it is my picture, and then you must place it by Tara's. You must walk into Bollywood House, naming for customers every star. You must stay, remembering all this is yours. We cannot take our wealth with us, wherever we go. It is here, it is here, to share. This is my recipe under every recipe, the only truth a father tells a child he has reaped. The tartest kordoi of all.

Kordoi Khar

1 ripe papaya

2 kordoi

2 clove of garlic

1 green chili

1 tablespoon khar ("baking soda" made from banana peel ash)

  sugar and salt to taste

1–2 tablespoons mustard oil

1. Heat oil in pressure cooker.

2. Add crushed garlic and chili.

3. Dice and add papaya and kordoi.

4. Add kola khar and mix "black" base thoroughly.

5. Add sugar and salt to taste.

6. Add 2–3 cups water and let simmer until two or three whistles.

7. Normally served at the start of a course, khar may be eaten for an upset stomach.

JUMI

Back in the Bronx! Spring too, so dogwoods on our parkway sprout gold. Heat in the air, black boys loping in loose jeans, Boricua girls strolling in bright tanks, the long-ing-ting of bachata. Baba sings over Bhupen Hazarika the whole way till we pull into the driveway, *buku hum hum kore . . . my heart quivers . . .* he always has this sweetly scratchy sound.

He slams the car door and kneels by a bulbous orange flower. Gently, he pinches it off and tucks it behind my ear. "Go get a bowl. We'll pick some for the *puja* tonight."

I sit on a white bedsheet on the living room floor as the House comes. Dorji Uncle hands out *saa* in Styrofoam cups, which steam the room, while Vikas sets the Geeta on Ma's old xorai. Imraan Da lays bananas across that brass stand, places its cone top by the *taals*. They ruffle my hair and promise to play when I'm better

The other uncles come, from Manhattan, Queens, New Jersey. Most are slight, hard-jawed Assamese, some North Indians with elegant noses, South Indians with inky eyes, a few of different nations entirely. But all conjured at 7:00 p.m. from the train, the bus, their rental vans straight from work. They sit cross-legged, in white shirts and dark trousers, on this white sheet on the living room. They sip this tea from cups and wave me into their circle.

One by one, they lean over and pat my back, stroke my cheek, sweep down my braid. One by one, they set down their cups, rub their palms, begin clapping.

They hum.

In the circle's corner, my father settles near me and lifts his brass *taals* into the air. Slowly, he scrapes each large cymbal against the other.

Shh-ha-shh.

Then faster.

Krung-brr-krung.

Scrunching his slanted eyes, my father sings. Worn face lifted, voice reedy. Plaintive.

The men sing with him, roaring into chorus, clapping with those clanging brass *taals*.

One sad, steady tune after another, Sankar Dev prayers where everyone rocks back and forth around me.

My father stands and circles me, beating those *taals*, singing faster.

One by one, the men rise, trailing in a line behind him, the circle widening, singing louder.

In the center, I shiver, while the men step *side-side-forward* around me.

Slow twisting circle.

Under me, the floor shakes warm with their stomping.

Side-side-forward. Vibrating circle. Closing in on me.

My father crouches and rises, crouches and stays, cymbals clanging-scratching-breathing right at me.

Still, they sing.

All the while, I look not up at them but down. At the men's shadows bent, black, converging on me. My father's fiercest, quickest of all, hands nicked by other people's appetites, grinding the taals. My father, whose raw-boned face is the home I know, shuts his eyes. My father, my father, who has called up the men, can you call up the women? Can you call up the stars?

The Carnival

B razil, Brazil. The *ooo-le-le* of samba, *ah-vaya* of white sand beach, *biddibiddiboom* of russet hips. My nineteen-year-old self saw right through this postcard shit yet two years later, here I am! Back! I'm lurching in the rear of a garbage truck, between barrels of sour apple mush, pink houses with dogs, green humps that drift through fog. And I'm whistling an old Assamese tune about a tree, like half our folk songs are, watching for the old woman Anju. Yet again.

Nineteen when my Brazilian stepmother first sent me, Miss Bad Attitude from The Bronx. This was a ploy I called The Cheap Immigrant's Correctional: a chicken farm. This was also two months after the sangría fest she and Dad called a wedding, where they foxtrotted like hot-and-knowing lovers, while I sat drinking White Russians like they were just milk. *That* was six months after Ma faded out, a human battery hooked and wired, corroded by a tumor those fat cat doctors couldn't find. "You'll love Brazil," my stepmother said my first summer night in from gray Boston U. "You'll never want to leave."

"Of course I won't," I said. "I'd have to see you again." That made Dad turn, shaking red. "Shut up and go."

Twenty-two now, and it's not like I know much more about where

I'm headed. I do know why—always have—but does self-knowledge really matter? The truck whistles—*halt*—nourishment in another town whose name only the towners know.

A carnival's here.

We spill out, grandmothers, honey farmers, blond-dreaded hippies, Indian girl me, into the balloon-and-light-speckled plaza. Men call out chicken roasted on sticks, grannies suck cobs on church steps, teens scurry past curtains of big-bottomed pretties, pot-bellied couples watch white-headed street kids leap from one grassy square to square. Spinning to see it all, I stumble on a step of kerchiefed ladies, who push gooey chunks of chocolate my way.

"You shouldn't eat so fast," a gray-eyed mister says, watching my mouth like he'd lick the cake right out of it. Maybe he knows I'm looking too, at his bulbous nose, his storkish bend beside me. "I'm Galego."

"Kabita," I say, and because his eyes creep up my jeans, I add, "I'm American."

"*Então,*" he says, taking my plate from me, "we must see the play."

I pull my wrist from his grasp—*can't! Anju!*—when what do I hear but her snappy pace on nights I wouldn't join her for bar dances. "Get out, *moça*. Live."

We walk past the chicken vendors to a dusty rotunda, where parents jostle to seat their kids on the rough brick edge. *Saudade, saudade* the actors sing, reaching with lean limbs and bronzed faces for a time they've never known, but the stamp of it there! Chirping Indians, they hop in file; swaggering Portuguese, they point their swords at limp Africans dragged in with ropes; then the pounding, of drums, against sprawled Indian legs, buckled African backs; and over a chorus of groans, the lyric call of babies.

"Look," a child whispers beside me to his mother. "*Você.*"

Galego presses my shoulder, but frowns at the coconuts flaking paint, papayas raining glitter, the oil-spilled waves on which the goddess Iemanja rides tilting like a Domino tile. Which is how I spot that bastard, cross-legged like a swami under the sharpest wave: Tonho of the piano teeth and piccolo heart.

Harh-harh, he laughs to the samba, clapping the cymbal hands he used to rap on Anju's gate for nothing good. Same old idiot, I bet, who'd woo a woman ninety pounds smaller, twenty years older with wildflowers and cheap chocolates, then yell at her for burnt *feijão*, thwack her into the cracker bin. The sort who'd toss moto-cyclist cash on cards, then come stumbling in for midnight mommy love. All those nights I scrubbed his beer and pee from the glistening floor while Anju pleaded and groaned behind the blue bedroom door! I repeated in my sleeping bag what I'd murmured on the Bronx couch, nights Mom wept on the iced stoop while Dad snored. *Maybe this is how love sounds for them.* And I knew, no one would risk his hide in these backways for an old woman and a foreign girl.

Dawn, after Tonho had vroomed off on his moto-taxi, I'd wander onto the porch to find Anju smoking corn husks from her stool. She'd shut her slanted eyes and suck that roll, so the pansies bloomed blue along her arm and neck. Then without a word, she'd bring wild tea out in a basin and wash the scalp I monkey-itched. This was the long black hair Ma had combed daily, which had, in her hospital days, tangled and thinned. More than Anju's hands plucking out my lice, I loved palm-oiling her fuzz, corn-rowing it into uneven furrows—though mornings after Tonho, she cringed with every tug. When I finally said Tonho had a temper, she sloshed the tea-water away. "If I want your opinion," she called from the kitchen, "I'll ask."

What I wanted was a clear number: for the value of a sixty-two-year-old chicken-raising Baiana's love, for the trade a forty-two-year-old Assamese woman keeping a Bronx house had made, laughter for life. I wanted one of them to tell me what price a nineteen-year-old Assamese American should pay—if love was ever worth it. But Ma's long gone, Zombie Dad's bewitched by StepBitch, and I've only got Anju's Broke Bad Boy, who might not tell me anything at all.

Tonho's staring at me—spooky eyes, no smile at all—but I step behind Galego. "Let's go!"

Galego widens his eyes, then clasps my hand down a dirt road, away from the plaza toward the parlors. All around us, trees darken into night, tents light up, and Galego rubs his thumb in circles on my palm. He doesn't blink at the signs glowing behind the chiffon— *Dança Exotica, Dança da Noite, Dança do Desejo*—doesn't even glance at the girls feathered and jeweled inside like Vegas birds. But I can't miss the wood shacks, cowering like dogs between the parlors, windows black and boarded. The girls who stroll there, winking and whispering at men, look so young—as if they should be in class with me—and so Indian—slender, dark-eyed daughters of Amazonians forced to move out here, somehow make it.

Rub-press-rub goes Galego's thumb, except he sings too, a buoyant Chico Cesar song about a man waiting for a love letter. *Why don't you snatch your hand up,* I wonder. *Run off like a frightened bunny? 'Cause,* I think as our road winds toward lights spinning up, *you're a curious cat.* And I go on, painting a life for this man whose name is the single thing I know, and even that, so uncertain. I paint for him a city wife, with jet-black hair and scarlet nails, who's left him for an agua de coco man on their street. I paint a seventeen-year-old daughter, caramel limbs camel-loping from bar stools to dance with strangers. I'd even paint a lover, a magic mountain woman maybe, but our road hits a carnival of fire.

All about a grassy clearing, costumed folk mill before tents strung with towels and shirts, behind fire-eaters, who toss up burning pins, spin lit hoops with swift hips. *We know,* they beckon with bony hands, *you wanna play.*

"You'll like my family," Galego says, stroking my left eyebrow, then my right. Dammit, I shiver—as kids dart from plastic-bound balls to the center fire, where two men cradle a drum, a guitar—he's right. The old man settles into a wheelbarrow, plucking a tinfooted melody, while the thumbless one presses his ear to skin, rippling nine fingers for a beat.

Flush-faced women swish out the shed, snapping fingers over their heads, prancing on quick feet to the fire. The one in purple draws near a man with the gold eyes and velvet skin of a Halloween cat, and when they hug their hips, Black Cat splays his gecko fingers on her smooth back, his braid beads clicking against her round cheeks. A brassy-chested redhead bounces before the musicmen, slapping her thighs, yelling at them to make it real, make her go. Men swarm about her, trying to cut in, match her pace, make her stick to them alone. But the old woman's the best, circling the fire like an epileptic, one palm waving, shoulders jiggling, a true magic mountain woman.

When I giggle, a blond boy holding a plate of clementines says, "That's my mother. Mamae!"

The old woman stumbles over, grasps the skinny shoulders of the boy, whose sudden grin warms the night. "Who is this street kid, José?"

I answer, "I'm looking for my Palmeiras friend. Anju da Silva."

"Why didn't you say so?" Galego says. "The road to Palmeiras is ruined from this year's rains. You won't find her on your own."

"I did before," I say, and thank my stepmother for her lucky mistake. She'd given Anju the wrong date, so I landed in the Salvador station early, waited all night for someone to come. Dawn, I rode the first bus to Palmeiras, hitchhiked to the only chicken farm towners knew was owned by a five-foot woman. There on the porch she crouched, tapping her cane at the chickens. "So you're the baggage."

"This wasn't my idea," I'd snapped, and she'd led me through a woodstove kitchen, past shelves of permaculture books, into a cool earth room with only a hammock and a cot. "Looks like you don't sleep in America," she said, pointing at the fresh sheets. I awoke sore, in an instant it seemed, Anju studying me from her hammock, by a window of corn.

"It's dark," Galego says, as if I were blind. "Stay the night and I'll help you find her tomorrow."

Magic Mountain Woman smiles. "Is this baby going to sleep with you, Galego?"

"She doesn't know anyone here!" Galego says.

Redhead strides over. "Are you two arguing over a woman again? Come! Let me decide!"

"Stay out of this!" Galego says. Sure enough, children scamper over, the musicmen amble up, plucking cheerful tunes.

"*Gente*," Redhead says. "Our troupe leader wants to sleep with a little girl. Why don't you hire a whore, Galego? Or do you want to save money tonight?"

Galego jumps for her, but José hugs his waist. "Right here," Redhead thumps her chest. "Come get it!"

Lord—I clap my palms over my eyes—*I'll never find Anju with these crazies.* I see Ma instead, bloodless face turned away that last week. Still, I had whispered to her not to leave me in the house alone, and held her hands that did not press back. Until she'd turned to sigh. "Now you will know how it feels."

One sunburst week later, Assamese folk streamed into the hall Dad rented, and I clapped my mother's soul up to a heaven I didn't believe in, repeated the prayers of a man I could've chopped and strewn in the toilet. But he sat, a pretend lama, circled by grave faces recounting a mother I hadn't known: joking, bustling, unlined. Not one of those good citizens mentioning the last years, when she'd called them sobbing, when she'd cowered at parties, sensing the whispers.

The house was emptied of her Indian bracelets, her rose water and oils, her hidden notes. *Our Lady of Mercy. November 5, 1985. Ten pounds, four ounces. Midnight, stained underwear in bathroom. June 2, 1997. Thirteen years old.* I hummed through it all—the neighbors who wouldn't look directly at me, the club clothes and car I wrecked, my As that bloated into Cs and Ds—as if song would chase anything away.

"I have traveled far!" a voice rasps. I drop my palms to Galego and Redhead staring at Magic Mountain Woman, who addresses the moon. The moon doesn't answer, so she spreads her arms to the huddled children, kneeling couples. "I am sixty-seven. Sixty-seven, *gente*, and I have never seen actors like you!"

She marches to the fire, talks to it instead. "We have talent. We have potential. We are doing the work given only to the inspired. And what," she whispers, "have we lowered ourselves to? Discord? The commonplace squabbles of artisans? Are we artisans?"

The audience nods.

"We are not!" Magic Mountain Woman says. "We must rise above these vulgarities! These distractions!"

She coughs and presses her chest. "Please, people. Don't upset me. *You*," she reaches out a hand, and when I move in, she slings an arm about my neck. She's more brittle than I imagined, like a sparrow that's flown into my sphere rather than the other way around. "I want this Indian girl to help me home."

Everyone's mum—except Galego, who kisses my forehead. "Take care," he says, as if forgiving me. Redhead scrapes her chair away, but Magic Mountain Woman could care less, limping out the clearing with the dignity of a queen, her Indian in tow. Only José trails us, like a yellow lizard scampering back to the loins of this earthy woman.

The road ahead winds to a cube as green and lit as Magic Mountain Woman herself. With every step, she hums a song I can't make out, and pinches my arm on beat. As if she were destiny reminding me: *You will borrow these women for restless nights. You will not keep a single one.*

⌒

I wake like I never do, to a house flush with sun. All bone and gray hair beside me is Magic Mountain Woman, breath like a baby's, opal hand warm against my chest. All night, she'd pressed her hand there, as if to heat up my heart, ground me in that solid bed. The precious thing about the old is their skin feels the way butterflies look. As I rub her loose skin over all her tiny joints, I feel like I'm lying under my mother's hand. Or Anju's.

But I'm a mover rather than a keeper, so I slip my feet to the cool earth floor. As I cross the threshold, I know I'm a lucky girl to be befriended by strangers.

Yesterday's road pierces the hill like a lifeline headed somewhere, so I trek the way I came, whistling all my mother left me, tunes Anju had muted herself to hear. Assamese la-las about Old Man River, the first blossoming tree, a daughter returning home. No one sings back—not a peep even from the camp, bundles asleep by the smoking pyres. Except for Galego, who's rocking and groaning under a blanket with Redhead. Good for her—and me, I guess.

I corkscrew downhill so robustly, even if it ends in a nothing-town, where folks set off for money-making vistas. Lonely cities of noise, sertões of thirsty poets, even jungles of Indians who may not look like me. I cross drying streams, I trespass rickety-gated farms, I backpack along a pink trail I hardly remember . . . this angle over the carnival plaza . . . that view of *peito da moça* . . . to the lowest slope of slippery terrace steps.

"Kabita!" someone says. Sneakers skid the last steps, then the grin from last night's coffee, then a blond ponytail. José: all of him and him alone.

He pants. "Mamae said you'd either burn down the hill or yourself."

"Fire wants water," I say. I lift the flask strung around his neck, and he slips *pão com queijo* out his pocket. Plopping in mud under ten o'clock sun, we crunch and suck crumbs off finger after finger.

José rests back on his elbows. "The rains ruined the crop. Most folks left for the city."

"She raised chickens," I say.

He turns onto his stomach and squints at me. "Even so."

I heave myself up into heat buzzing with birds, bees, and God knows what else. "I have to try."

"Then why," José says, re-climbing the terrace steps, "are you going the wrong way?"

We walk again up the hill, on the terraced pink path that seems worn now and watchful. Flanked by Bible boulders, the tiniest birds zipping between bushes, how old is this road really?

The first time I'd spotted a hummingbird, I could've touched the fleshed jewel, darting about a red hibiscus by my ear.

"Beija-flor," Anju said. "Our most precious thing."

This was the first real sentence she'd spoken, and I stood mute till the kiss-flower flashed away.

We'd hiked on, four hours for a waterfall she said she could feel. *What waterfall, where waterfall, you broke hag?* I thought whenever she paused to tap her cane about. But we found water under a low cliff, a gurgling column hidden by crooked trees. Like a grinning imp, Anju stripped and sidled into the water, while I clutched a pineapple for dear life.

"You waiting for the bus, *menina*?" she yelled. "This is good for your spirit."

One spirit conjures another, for who whistles toward us but Tonho, fedora cocked on his stupid head, a starved dog dragging over gravel behind him.

"I thought I saw you," he says.

"You know why I'm here," I say.

"Are you with her?" he asks José, who's frowning at the metal chain wound thrice around the dog's neck.

Dear José puffs out his chest. "Our whole troupe is looking for her friend."

Tonho assesses my reddened face, my caked jeans, maybe even the ending to my trip. I want to throttle him: *What's the big fucking deal? I'll pay you if you want. I'll even apologize for nothing. Just hand her over!* But I eye him back, not a muscle twitching. I know how to play this game.

Tonho turns, yanks the dog back up the terraced road. "I don't know where she is. A lot of folks ditched Palmeiras after the rain destroyed their homes. Some things were left in the church."

Another half-hour, we hit the next leveled cliff, where a colonial with white adobe walls moons over a speckled oval. The town—and beyond it, brown fields I'd blurred, except in stabbing moments, about as well as Ma's face. What the tourist books called dryland and Anju *a minha poema do sertão.*

"Don't just stand there," Tonho says, rattling the blackened door.

José holds my hand past wood pews, over a floor swirling with circles, as if someone were welcoming us. But it's the ceiling holes, plugged with broken bottle bottoms, that greet us while candles flicker by photos, all along the sides. Photos and ribbons and notes.

I turn—surprise, surprise—Tonho's gone, as suddenly as that last week, when I'd crept over to Anju huddled in bed. *Everyone,* she'd said when I kissed her wet cheek, *leaves.*

"Kabita," José says as he sifts through burlap bags lined before a gold-gilded altar. As if the people had hoarded their faith in that altar, and those bags, from which José pulls leather sandals, silver bangles, cracked photos of stiff families. Then I pause his hand— "Her crystals!"—a blue kerchief knotted around small stones.

I unwrap the silk, spilling pink-white jags onto my palms, which I lift to his bright blue eyes. "My first day here, the kids took me to a hill where they collected these. I told them they were just rocks but they said, 'No. These are real and precious.' They gave me everything they found. My last week, I took Anju to that hill, told her we'd look together."

"Did she believe you?" José says.

"It hadn't rained that summer so the hills were dark." I point to the holes in the stained glass behind the altar, brown grass peeking through. "She said she was glad we'd come. That I'd see how green the land could be after the rain."

José ties one sack after another, and only after the last burlap's lined up does he say, "It's half a day's ride from here."

I don't know if he means we should or shouldn't go, so I say, "I can't."

"Where else have you got to go, *princesa*?"

I'm on the town road one last time, José muttering how the troupe will flog him if he returns empty-handed. But even with José whistling to birds he names, or naming hills cleared of fog, the roads seems rockier, winding to the same ol' hub of strangers. No friend there.

Dusk, we're rattling on a bus past the deep green mounds, toward a planet of brown stalks, burnt stumps. We can't help staring out the window at the dusty road, haunted by dark figures who don't glance back. "*Poxa!*" José says, and I remember when I too marched in blistery sandals. How I'd thumbed for a *carrona* and muttered to Anju about hell. How she'd shuffled on, as if already dead.

My midday bread burns my chest, and when I turn gulping, José puts a warm finger to my throat and grins. Those buck teeth—I roll back to the window and shut my eyes to all that tan, tan, tan . . . and dream of concrete sidewalks Ma and I wandered, hand-in-hand. Long hair wound into a moon the men watched, she speaks Assamese only we know. "Kabita, your name means poem; Kabita, what do you want to eat?; Kabita, we'll walk around once, before your father gets back." The bus jolts—*para!* folks yell—José brushes a strand from my eye. "Ten minutes."

The caatinga's nothing if not a spread of cautious hearts, thorn trees twisting up dry bark, pale green cacti throwing long shadows. But the rain that's razed Palmeiras has woken this thistle-patch, and these wry citizens show their treasures. Feathery stars splash earth, still butterflies swell cacti branches. Gold wildflowers bloom between white rock, and spattered all over the moist soil, a hundred deep prints. Deer, lizard, bird.

"Try this," José says, carving with a pocketknife sap that must've leaked and dried onto a knobby tree.

As I chew the rubbery knot, I remember my last night, Anju's friends gathered in the caatinga to bid me safe goodbye. Earlier that evening, she'd slung a bloody plastic bag on her wood stove, and smiled. "The heart of your friend." My first day, I'd told her good Hindu girls didn't eat beef, but learned over the weeks, *sertanejos* saved every scrap. Especially, the tough, tender *coração*. "I'll watch you all," I joked back.

How the crackling heart shot sparks that night, as Anju's friends talked land.

"MST's no better than the government," Old Man Fiel said. "I'll believe them when they give me more than dirt I can hold in my hand."

"Should we give up?" Anju said. "This could be our chance."

Ines, nursing her dark shiny baby, shifted it left. "You have your plot, Anju. Most of us can't sit on the roadside for land we deserve but won't get."

"What does our American think?" Fiel said.

Silly that I was, I'd been watching the heart drip juice into the fire, sizzling spice up. "Huh?"

"What *would* an American think?" Anju said.

I wanted to jump atop my stool, speechify for every American immigrant.

I'd clear my throat: everyday, my father walked barefoot from his village to school, after waking at dawn to till the rice fields.

I'd shout: my mother mopped and vacuumed the same brick house for eighteen years, on Bronx blocks where no one spoke her language.

I'd pump my fist: my parents gave up new coats and socks to pay for college. Other than India, they'd never even left the Bronx.

But Anju's strained face, all those wizened faces made my story hollow. These folks didn't want to leave the hills. Most days, they wore no shoes at all.

Brilliantly, I answered, "I don't have American opinions!"

The circle blinked while Anju turned the spit. "It's ready."

Murmuring broke the chilly air, blankets rustled, forks clinked out—and Anju passed maroon slices out on plates that, when I shook my head, kept going round. But as Anju licked the tip of her meat, as everyone sucked oily fingers and sighed, I thought, *I'd like a piece of the heart too.*

José rests a hand on my shoulder. "Everyone's expecting us."

I walk away, old Abraham in desert, Rama exiled for who he was, until I reach a stout tree with a hole the size of my head. Stuffing the crystals into the hole, I think, *Here is one of the loveliest places no one knows to die.* My mother burned far from the betelnut village she knew, in a Bronx funeral home; Anju's gone who-knows-where, only stones left to her caatinga; while I'm too lost a thing to know how my fate will end.

"Stay with us," José says, slashing through a tangle of vines. "At least for a while." He leans against the tree, blocking the hole. "Some troupe job will keep you."

Which would only prove my folks right: *stubborn freak, wayward girl, good riddance.* But if I'm never right, I may as well feast my own heart out.

"Let's see," I say, and turn to the bus roaring for the others. Strangers who've come from unknown towns for their own strange reasons. Wanderers who climb slowly on board, to return to carnival that's throbbed up once more. The tents, the fires, the dancing folks. We will pass from this living land to the next, and without words, with eyes open, we will wish. To go further, to rest a bit, then press on.

Mufaro's Beautiful Daughter

The year my father built his Zerega house—a two-story ram-shackle with mirrors for walls and fake marble chips in the rose beds—was the year I joined my storytelling contest. It was my mother, really, who pushed me that way, but it was my fifth-grade teacher who was right. Your destiny was laid out for you, if only you chose to read the signs.

My father, plunging the toilet, complained early on that she had picked "Mufaro's Beautiful Daughters" because she was black. My mother, wiping the tile sludge around him, declared, "You sound like an Indian girl telling a Xhosa story in a Bronx accent." But in her sun-washed classroom every afternoon, Mrs. Chapman wound her hair into a bun and reassured me it didn't matter what I read, so long as I told it right.

So every night, as my father hammered those mirrors into walls, I orated to sea critters I imagined in the basement; and all week-end, as my mother held a flashlight over him, I thumbed through fairytale books for girls like me. Storytelling Scheherazade, lost li'l Thumbelina, and the surprise Princess and her surprise Pea. Even my parents, who could recite Wordsworth poems and name forty

Ahom kings, batted the Funny Mystery of Me over the marigolds they were digging.

"The teacher," my mother muttered, "called Nirmali shy in class, wild at recess."

My father tapped his forehead. "The daughter of Buddha will do great things in the world."

"The hospital," my mother declared, "gave us a demon child."

My father glared at her. "Our last name means 'dynasty of king.'"

"Sure," my mother said, handing me a trowel, "we're royalty."

What *were* we doing, living on a Lydig block of old Jews, midway between the white Italian mafia houses and the highrise clothes-lines that fluttered panties and Puerto Rican flags? Why were we fixing a dirty brick house we weren't going to keep, that we meant to sell to the only sort of people who'd move to Zerega, black and brown? My why-bother-to-reply parents fretted over the three hall-way arches instead—turtling one week per arch—giving up when the wood cost more than they expected. *It's okay*, they told each other about that last unframed arch. *Buyers would remember what they saw first.* But I thought, *no*, even with my crooked eyes, I'd notice the plain arch, the way the fancy front made the naked back look bad.

My father pointed me to the mirrors and grunted, "Go watch yourself talk." He never noticed how I tripped over the toolbox, how I pressed against the glass to focus the tears zigzagging down my cheeks, how I heard my girlfriends' dirty chanting over my hum-drum words. Aboard the public school bus, they had drawn stick figures undressing and doggie humping. The fact that two people would go through all that trouble only to regret me meant I *was* out-of-this-world.

Dragging my books back into the mirror-doubled dark didn't help, and I was left tracing irrelevant details: colored pencil draw-ings of brown bodies and birds, pages that went from gardens to thatched huts to carved chambers, the brash laugh when Mrs. Chapman had glimpsed my storytelling face.

"Quit squinting," she'd said. "You look like a gnome."

"How can I tell who I'm talking to?" I'd asked.

"You should be listening to yourself," she'd replied. "Tell your parents to drop by."

When I stumbled to the porch with this news, I tipped my father's cinnamon-steeped tea off the rail. Zinnias sizzling, my father cursed me off and my mother dragged me to the mirrors. There— sturdy jungle heathen beside her trim ivory form—I wondered *who* I belonged to. Until my mother wryly noted, "Your father also knocks things around." Then I saw myself shudder, I heard myself laugh.

❧

My mother doesn't call anymore and, these four years, neither have I. Every day, nine to five, I teach clients how to speak from their gut rather than their throat, but I clench my own voice in fists behind my back. When my clients wisecrack that they barely hear me, I remember my mother screaming the last time we talked.

"I never wanted children! Look how you've turned out! I have nothing to say to people when they ask!"

Like so many times, a steak knife lay on the table between us. Sobbing, I clutched the steel and crawled on all fours into the corner. I sliced apart my shirt, my breasts falling out like spheres with plum centers. "Stop!" I said. "Please stop!"

My mother rose and rinsed the dishes. I crawled again and lay my head on her warmed seat. "Look at me," I said. "Is this what you want?"

"I don't want anything," she said, thumping off the tap.

Weeks later, my mother's vessels dripped into her retinas, so that it wasn't a choice of not seeing me. So that both of us saw only straight ahead: she to her first job in public housing, me to coaching immigrants who couldn't speak. But my father, who calls most afternoons, cites every mile, every possibility as crisply as ever. He barks over the train from the burbs, where he reminisces about all things Oxomiya with some uncle over tea. I listen for what he doesn't name, doctors pumping blood from his legs up to his heart. EECP, meaning this is the best stalling tactic my fading Deeta can afford.

"I found a voice coach job in New York," he said the last time. "You don't have to live in Manhattan. You can live in the Bronx."

"I like California," I said. "It's peaceful. I have friends here."

My father paused, hearing maybe what I wouldn't admit. How, nightly, I bike by sprinklers in this parched valley, dream of dark, lucid eyes that truly see me, long for his sweetly-tipped lids most of all. How, every morning, I stare at a phantom I can't reach through glass. My father mumbled then that he and my mother are house-hunting again. They want to live in the borough's east end, by the boats and bridges and upper middle class folk.

"The neighborhood's no good anymore," he said. "Too many wild elements."

"I like that about it," I said. "I'll miss it."

I will—though I used to pray for the day I'd leave Lydig, used to think, when I landed in Davis, I'd walked clear through the earth. Everywhere, limber palms, broad-armed shrubs, firs that dropped resiny cones, blue wildflowers that looked like they'd come from the mountains. Why, every morning, I'd wake on a lumpy cot in a poorly-plumbed house and know I never wanted to leave. Why, most evenings, I pack dirt around alyssum, thyme, and sage in a rocky plot. Humble plants I chose because they could handle the heat, grew even between rock. But after three years of drought and a green thumb I didn't inherit, my flowers wither into brown curls.

Today, I ask my father how he made zucchini vine over the rails, mint shoot up and scent the deck. Every sunset, we knelt together, watering bright tomatoes, spiny cucumbers.

"The stupid squirrels ate everything," he says. "The tree blocks all the sun."

My father climbed, before his heart surgeries, the old elm to its quivering top. He'd hack off new branches, push out squirrel nests, straddle down with the knife between his teeth. Now, he won't risk breaking bones for fear he won't last another operation. But the elm carresses our Lydig windows, squirrels skirmishing along its branches.

"Ma fried zucchini flowers in besan," I say, remembering their sweet petals, their bitter innards.

"Come home," he says. "You're missing her cooking."

I hope he doesn't know what else I've chosen to miss. Their faces furrowed like plains, bamboo art that whispers off every wall, morning calls in village tones I'll never get. All of it lodged in a heart I've failed to bury. So that even dreamless nights, I see. Faces as dark and brooding as dusk, graffiti art that jumps you from every corner, nightly shouting in a hundred languages I'll never know. All those rough edges. All that nervy life.

⤚

Indian summer bloodied the parkway and still, I said nothing to my folks about my eyes or to Mrs. Chapman about my folks. My father was tearing up the red carpet for imitation wood while Mrs. Chapman was nailing the "t"s into my prim street lingo. When my mother finally painted the Zerega rooms canary yellow, Mrs. Chapman lent me her owl-frames and marched me before the district judges.

Always, those grimsters were a fuzz from the podium where, shot with some cocktail of panic-n-pluck, I squeaked high and quick. I survived in this Minnie Mouse way for several rounds, beating out kids who sounded like Darth Vader, who forgot key lines like "once upon a time" and "happily ever after," who peed right before they cried their way to the end. By the time October stripped the oaks, Mrs. Chapman pumped her fists and announced, I'd made the borough meet; did I want to go? *Sure*, I said, hugging her wasp waist and this extra secret from my parents, who swept brittle leaves from the Zerega stoop rather than our Lydig one. What did I have to lose?

For better or worse, I discovered an elevated torture, enacted not in another dark auditorium but in the septic library of P.S. 68. Its full-on lights revealed what I knew too well, those clenched immigrant jaws—Italian, Jamaican, Filipino—my parents' sandpapered planes suddenly among that wary terrain. What were they doing here, hands folded on laps, eyes fixed on my good denim dress? Had Mrs. Chapman, spry figure wired in the front, said something?

I gulped—*focus, focus*—and counted the heads in the line twitching before me. Twelve, then ten, then six . . . Alice by Alice—*off with their heads!*—felled by fickle adults. Removing my dud glasses, I listened to the still-standing band: brassy notes of a Jamaican boy reading "Anansi the Spider," nervous piccolo of a Vietnamese girl reading "Three Perfect Peaches," nasal oboe of a Jewish girl reading "Baba Yaga." And as I too shuffled before the beige blur, my heart *thump*-thumped.

How could it possibly win this rat race? Hell, how'd it even get this far?

For ten minutes, I read without breath and without flaw. According to rules, anyways, on posture and elocution and all those fancy words Mrs. Chapman had repeated, not a single syllable saying anything about the heat of Mufaro's land or the salt in his beautiful daughters. I sounded like a misplaced parrot. Why *was* I talking about spirited Xhosa royals in this faux-British accent to slight wayfarers staked stubbornly in a library? Who was *I* to tell folks, who'd left jungles of guns and muddy luck, about savannahs of princes and palaces, none of which I'd seen?

Yet I recited, how Nyasha, the sweet sister, befriended everyone and won the heart of the king, disguised as a garden snake all along. How Manyara, the nasty sister, dismissed every cue the spirits gave her—hungry forest boy, man carrying his head under his arm—and served Nyasha when she turned queen. But my heart whispered to my head: Manyara was gutsy, she was smart. She'd run all night, from the only home she'd known, for love and wealth; she'd clashed with the five-headed snake king, then warned her sister not to risk him. And why wasn't washing her sister's feet, that goody two-shoes who never said no, the humblest devotion?

The judges huddled with other whispers, pronouncing me the girl with the trophy, the girl with the clay heart. So when people clapped, I bowed, and when my father swung me up, I grinned. Until Mrs. Chapman walked up and said, "She gets dizzy."

"Thank you," my mother said, slipping the owl-frames off my sweaty nose, "but she doesn't need handouts."

Mrs. Chapman unbuttoned her blue blouse collar. "Can I offer you a ride?"

She lingered before the chipped brick of our Lydig front, Queen Anne's lace spurting from the cracks. My mother, without another thank you, dragged my father up the concrete steps.

"See you tomorrow?" I said.

Mrs. Chapman frowned as if unsure whether she taught on a weekday, whether she taught odd-eyeballed kids at all.

"I'll hide the glasses," and I kissed her cheek before scampering to the Lydig door. By then, her blue Camry had turned the corner, so I squinted down the hallway at my parents. Their shadows, murmuring, hunched away, as if I were the stranger.

ᝣ

I keep my sister a secret in Davis, though everywhere else I've run to—Boston, Salvador, Guwahati—I've sung odes about her. I would've jumped in front of a truck to save her, given her a kidney if she needed it, fist-fought with any man who dared hurt her. That was how I stopped talking to my father for a year, the only family I believe in anymore, the one person I trust truly loves me.

Who remembers how fights begin? Only indestructible details: my father a bellowing bull at the edge of the living room, my sister pleading and shrinking into a littler girl against the stairs. I strode in from the kitchen and slammed a bowl of yogurt on the couch, splattering the sour white across our feet. "Stop screaming at everyone what to do!" I don't like to remember what happened next, so I'll just say, there was some pounding, some bawling, and my mother and sister watching offside, moving not at all to save me.

I ran out on the streets for the hundredth time that night, wondering how far I could go without money, what my life would be like without family, if I'd get maimed in a different way out here. Several times, I walked all the way to Co-op City, the borough's north end, where we'd bus an hour to school. Other times, I walked to Orchard Beach, wishing I could mermaid into Long Island Sound or soar off with the black cormorants, the green herons. The iciest days, I hid among the weeds of our Lydig yard, waiting till the cops came and went, till my sister whispered my name from the deck.

Always, I walked back into that stone-cold cube. Not because I wanted to but because I didn't know where I was headed. Because I feared what would burst inside the only family I had in the only hood I knew. Because I wasn't sure which girl I was, the one whose name meant shame or the one whose name meant mercy. Because I sensed, walking the buoyant crayon streets, I'd find my way to my real home outside: brick buildings rising over chain-link fences, parking lots of maple and Indian grass, brown folks glancing at me with caution and with care. Why now, when square Davis faces raise their careful brows, their light eyes—*you poor thing in the dirty, dangerous Bronx*—I remember what no one says. How those streets gave me back my soul, kept the parts of my heart that hadn't been seized, saved the real life I didn't know I possessed underneath.

Every time I crawled back into bed, my sister sobbed and hugged me. "Promise," she'd mutter into my neck, "not to leave." Or, if she'd done her homework and mine, she'd ask, "Wanna play Snakes and Ladders? Wanna watch an Indian movie?" What she was doing in her downtime—in the bathroom, carving her wrists, the insides of her thighs, in the bedroom bartering with a God she didn't think was there, to save me before her—I glimpsed twice. When I spat at my mother—"You have no idea what's going on with Henna"—my mother widened her glassy eyes but kept them fixed on the VCR she was untangling.

These days, my sister calls me twice a year, never when I need her most, something more mysterious than a continent between us. She runs tests in a Chicago lab late into her weekend nights. "Humans have almond clusters in their brains," she says, "where they store emotion and memory." *People store a lot of things,* I want to say, *in the body.* And though I don't say what, we pause, reviewing the data the laboratory of our life handed us: what bruises chair legs leave when sisters ram them into each other, the way a father looks strangling a mother on a newly upholstered couch, the dramatic relief of sirens in your driveway, the rising tension as cop boots plod through your kitchen and out of your house.

৶

The gift I got Christmas morning, in my Lydig bed, was two busted eyes (and a sparrow in a blurry tree). Rooftops and roads beyond, which I'd known like the cut of my palms, had become one reckless smudge against a gray sky. Signs and strays, scattered in every grassy lot, had morphed into blots and dashes I couldn't name. I stretched, claws out. I was one more cat who'd have to hone her other senses to survive. My paws creaked the twelve steps to my mother's pithas, where I discovered my mouth. My tail peeled the banister to the car, where I jolted with every stop my father nearly missed.

Yet even in Zerega, lights strung around white dolls so it looked like a holy nursery, I didn't meow. My parents were trying to pitch the house. But when the Puerto Rican hairdresser, who wanted to set up shop in the basement, called it musty, I heard the *split! splat!* of the rusting pipes. When the Guyanese family complained the concrete yard was too small for their barbeque, I scraped my limbs dervishing into the rosebush. Only the African American grand-mother with the clouded eyes traced the slits between the mirror walls, the thorns leading to the roses, the gravel that ended at the lone tree. There I perched, nibbling a fig, but she caught my big toe with her fingers. "Does this cutie pie come with the place?"

For an incredible moment, I thought my parents might say, "Yes, ma'am! And we'll throw in a solid oak armory!" I imagined them investing the blood money in a rundown house they'd reshingle and replumb, where they'd live far more happily ever after without me. But when I said, "I wanna play," and pounced at her feet, the grandmother crinkled her eyes and laughed.

Still, I listened from the dank basement as my parents bartered with this pleasant voice that guarded one figure all afternoon. I listened harder when, after conceding to her price, my parents pulled my report card from the bill pile. A silence as round as those Cs filled the newly sold house. Where would Mystery Girl Losing Sight of Things go from here?

To the Parent-Teacher lounge the next evening, where Mrs. Chapman flitted her hummingbird hands in explanation.

"Nirmali can't see the board. But I don't think that's the only reason she's daydreaming. I was hoping you folks could tell me what's going on."

My father frowned at my mother, who muttered, "Why don't you ask her?"

I wandered to the windowsill, where I heard girls pattering double Dutch in the playground. They'd shifted my TV box to this window, and I peered in at the quails warbling on their molted fluff. For the past week, the chicks had been flapping their stiff new wings, so I'd taped wire gauze over the top. Still I wondered, every night in bed, which baby at rosy dawn would peck through the cardboard and run out? Which baby would I find tomorrow, broken and mute, roasted in the radiator or decapitated in a pencil sharpener?

"She's like this at home," my father said.

"Sometimes," Mrs. Chapman said, "the smart ones get bored or the sensitive ones withdraw. But I don't think that's Nirmali's problem. Aside from storytelling, she won't talk."

"But she excels at storytelling," my mother said.

"You folks don't get it," Mrs. Chapman said. "She can't even see her story anymore. You should've gotten her checked a long time ago. But that wouldn't have been efficient, would it?"

My parents cowered, glaring at Mrs. Chapman with the angry eyes of thieves. I wanted to wind past the desks and cry, *They're good people! Don't talk like that to them!* But I sank beside that cardboard box, and heard the girls chanting to their snapping ropes. And in some new corridor of my throat, my high heart palpitated: *your avenger has come.*

⤶

I still dream of endings that could be mine. Outcast girls who lose their way and die, wives stolen when tempted beyond the magic circle, daughters chopped and reborn in no man's garden. Though I've returned my mother's books—*Hans Christian Andersen, the Ramayana, Burhi Aair Sadhu*—I've carried those endings like chips in my side. From semi-detached Lydig to Tudor-faced Zerega, through rickety brick bargains to this Davis back alley.

You mean the chip on your shoulder, boyfriends will say, their fingers hesitating at ridges on my neck, wrists, thighs. *My side*, I'll say, pulling their fingers to smiles in the curve of my waist. My rich white boyfriend pulled away, as if I were deformed, as if scars were contagious. My African gambler boyfriend rolled right over, mimicking me and calling me a spoiled American. My North Indian boyfriend, who'd joked Assamese people were half-elf, half-hobbit, I didn't tell at all. Only my Cambodian refugee boyfriend kissed my scar and, for that alone, I miss him.

I told him half-stories both of us could bear. That I couldn't remember why my sister was cursing, if I had struck my mother first, if my sister threw that plate to defend her. I swore to him I wasn't sure what else I'd done wrong, confessed that maybe we all deserved it, that perhaps some families are meant, like sleepwalkers, to crash through things. What I did remember—more clearly than the slash of their eyes, the pale of their faces, the afternoon light boxing the floor, the pink button-down I was wearing—was the way we stood. A faux chandelier split us into camps, my mother and sister tensed forward in the hall, my back rigid against the front door. What I could name—more fluently than *KochKalitaKamrupi*—were the words we slung at each other. *Uncivilized, bitch, dummy*, we shouted in English. *Mok mari pelai diya*, we wept in Assamese.

"Is that how come you hate pink?" he'd asked.

Who knows why people hate anything? What I do know is the plate shattered into tiny pieces. Slivers the length of my pinky nail pierced my side, and feeling an itch, I rubbed the pieces in, grazed them under and up my skin, smeared blood I couldn't at first see. I was busy stumbling back, daring my mother, my sister to throw something else at me. They did—a cup that broke its handle against my rib, a fork that speared my nipple, a spatula that branded my calf—and I wept my way to the dining room radiator, where I crouched between the rubber plant and the lucky bamboo. I wept for a half-hour before my mother, coming over to say *shut up*, saw my newly red shirt, tried hugging me, dragging me by my arm to the tub.

My last boyfriend never asked why the way the others did. Never said a word when I said, "Because I'm my father's daughter. Dark, wild, mad." "That's crazy, you aren't," the other boys said, spitting out the diamond-hard truth. Love leaves marks, crazy is relative, some people come to prefer the bang-up job, especially if it's the closest thing they know. My last boyfriend simply gathered me to his own dark chest the long, warm night.

Now, my Cambodian gone, my father talks about my sister's wedding. "To a nice Indian boy, an engineer too, a good family."

He's building the mandap where they will sit, two couples beside the sacred fire.

"Will you be there?" he says, and I wonder if this is his voice or my mother's.

"How can you ask that?" I say, and remember Henna and I bride-grooming in the vast Zerega house. Rooms of sawdust and staples became banquet halls of champagne and guests. There we wrapped moldy curtains about ourselves into saris and tuxes. We snipped marigolds from our father's garden for our true love bouquets. We played old Hindi tapes on the boom box for our wedding marches.

Always, at the end of some hodgepodge Christian-Hindu rite, we hovered toward each other for the finale kiss.

"She's still my sister," I tell him. And for a moment, I see, as clearly as I used to, the roiling sea of Henna's face. Which is my own, a little lighter, just as open-and-shut. Eyes scrunched, lips puckered, expectation glistening on her tongue.

ᔦ

My parents waited till the morning of the final to give me my glasses, bulletproof squares I finally slipped on in some nameless park. Suddenly, the penguins plucking classical on the lawn turned into lean Jews cradling violas. The pointillist mist cleared into bow-tied judges and hatted mothers gliding under a striped tent.

Still, I could feel the weight of the sinking sun, and sweated into the darkest corner to stuff my mouth. All us immigrant kids had congregated—to slog down sparkling cider and gorge on chocolate-covered strawberries—and to watch the border of the tent. Dandelions and dogwoods had spilt gold all around us, on streets sizzling with summertime skirts, beneath cars blaring hip-hop poetics. Every block simmered with *oye! amor,* boiled over with dark bodies gleaming for beach, a resurrection we rushed out yearly to witness. Though this once, we couldn't trespass past the white tent spikes. We were made up too nice, combed and suited.

Supposedly frothing to speak, to tell our stories for ten minutes on a wood podium.

Three of us were left: the Jamaican spider boy, me the African princess Indian, and then there was Cassandra. Cassandra Pashupati, an Energizer bunny of a twelve-year-old who'd won the city title two years straight. Like her namesake, this high-class storyteller was a hard-to-believe legend. Despite her melodramatic gesturing, her tic that made her push up her glasses, her choked sobs when some other story pushed hers to second, she'd always pulled through to the final. Her story alone won in the end. No wonder we worried—until, of course, we met the Blessed One herself—and then we were paralyzed. With fear. With awe. With envy.

When she entered the tent, dressed in a flouncy white dress that was almost a Sunday school outfit, it was like running into my stunt double. My better twin. Not only was Cassandra Indian, she was more put together, more confident than I'd ever be. Flashes went off as she trotted, her better side angled to the audience, to her front row seat, a posse of mother-father-sisters-male cousins-galore trailing her. She patted her slick black bob, X-ray scoped me and the Jamaican, licked one forefinger before flicking each page of "Thumbelina." Already, I could hear my mother if she won. *You should've practiced more. Why didn't you act it out? Don't you know what charm means?*

But if someone had asked me, I would've said, I *liked* my understated, precise manners. Cassandra was a parody like, say, Dolly Parton. Someone might've said, but you love Dolly, and Cassandra seduces her audience, even reluctant little you. And I'd admit: when Cassandra marched up front, clasped her hands behind her back—FLASH—turned on like a high-voltage billboard in Times Square, I paid attention. To her toothy grin, wide fluttering eyes, swiveling head that met every face in the room. *You! Yeah, I'm telling this story to you!* But I would've added: her voice, somewhere between a bird's rich trill and a tree frog's plaintive croak, sounded forced to me. As if she too were storytelling for her life.

I'll admit also: I could've beat Cassandra, who stuttered twice, mixed the toad and the mole, called Thumbelina "Tumble-ina." Hell, she read the story of a homeless girl, bandied between animals who tried to marry her, as if orphanhood were bursting with positive energy. But I knew where the poetry lay: in Thumbelina's silences, the broken-winged swallow she tended in secret, the strangers who helped her as she floated through landscapes, looking for home. I could've even beat the Jamaican, who read as perfectly as a robot, the life spooked out of him by the crowd. Not a single laugh for all those great trickster lines.

But I lost. From stage, I crystal-balled a dozen blemishes on a hundred faces, my parents' coal eyes and Mrs. Chapman's whitened smile looming up front. Could they see me as I saw them? All those afternoons, I had read fairy tales, I had not noticed the red rims of my father's eyes, the sag of my mother's pretty cheeks, the way my teacher's left hand clutched her throat, as if she too wanted to speak but couldn't. Instead of asking what had led them to their expressions, under this tent, I had memorized a royal savannah that belonged to no one I knew.

A judge thumped his pencil, but I looked past his back row to the street beyond the tent. Beyond its row of twelve saplings, to the silhouette of road against brick against gloaming sky, a cobweb more vast and complicated than any Anansi might spin. I did not know what to call these roads that had led to this gussied-up park, but I saw how they ran past the tallest buildings, round the dingiest lots, spiking right into the red sun before it blazed out. I guessed at all the suns these roads would cross on the way to how many towns, and what strange moons they, like Manyara, would witness. All I had to do, to name streets that had always run by me, was walk them.

But first business first, I made up a story right there and then.

The Fabulous Sequel to Thumbelina, I said. *Her Adventures Part
II*. I don't remember what the hell I babbled, just the sounds as I
stared at those faraway streets: people flipping through programs
that gave a different title, the Jamaican's name, *Robert Jewles*, when
he won, my parents hissing at each other in the car, and Mrs. Chapman, who was quiet in the backseat, holding me, her heart going
pitpatpit into my face.

↜

"Tonight's gonna be fun!" Brook cries, running out in her *punk rock
chick* undies while I set a bag of old books down in Aster's kitch-
en. It's a play-date once Aster leaves, me cutting up Brook's salmon,
munching seaweed she feeds me, rubbing her down with lavender
oil. Then the ritual: spooning under a quilt embroidered with her
Indian name, *Shakti*, reading into her ear the way my mother read
into mine. How Nyasha and Manyara vied for a prince, how the
Wawalak sisters were reborn from a serpent, how Grimm sisters
were doomed to spill things whenever they spoke. One sister, flowers, and the other, frogs.

"I like frogs," Brook says, squirming round to assess me with her
brown button eyes. "Do you?"

"I don't know if I like them more than flowers," I say.

"Under water," she says, "they look like jewelry."

She wants Thumbelina last, insisting the pipsqueak travel to
stranger lands, visit weirder critters, hide in more exotic orchids.
For every detail I miss, she claps my mouth—"You forgot!"—till she
drools off in her curls, and Aster eases into the bedroom to find my
mouth clamped.

"False labor," she laughs, rubber-banding thyme and sage into my
purse. When I ask about her on-and-off dates with her off-the-rock-
er husband, she folds her hands. "I suddenly realized. My daughter
is my true love."

Is this true, I wonder as I bike about Aster's woodsy grounds, about mothers pushing daughters on swings, fathers catching sons off monkey bars, geese waddling after each other across grass. And I hear Brook's question, "Where's the Momma?" for every story that had none. *Immaculate male conception*, I wanted to tell the midwife's kid, but what do I know of life's miracle passages? Why my Tibetan friend points to the gap in her seven-year-old's grin and jokes, *The Gate of India*. Why my Assamese friend named her son *Neela Kantha*, after a god who, having drunk poison, got a blue throat but wouldn't die. Why my Kannada friend, a widow who calls her baby and dog her *traveling circus*, taught them *stop, good girl, I want.*

Or why my mother called this week, to ask about colors neither of us really see. She and my father are draping silk about the pillars of the altar, since Henna wants a royal look. When I say I hadn't heard but like purple, she cries softly, as if afraid someone might hear her.

"What happened?" she says.

"I couldn't answer that," I say, and she sobs. In hiccups, the way I do, nostrils probably pinched, the way mine get.

"This is a house of khong," she says, slipping into Oxomiya the way I will, when I weep behind knolls. Nights she cannot sleep, she says, she watches videos of Henna and me. Dancing, singing, sparring. My face flushes but I say nothing, and my mother switches to other things. How many times the altar fell, leaning too far left, too far right, how they found it in shambles each morning.

"Aji thakise. Finally," she says. "You know your Deeta. He doesn't give up."

I call my father as I yank up shriveled herbs, flowers, sticks. But his phone rings without end—he still can't set up a voice box—so I measure the broken fence encircling my upturned soil. When I'd first stepped through, I'd planned to set the jagged rails straight, buy a latch for the ghetto string. I'd learn all this when my father visited, so no matter where I lived, I'd be safe. But my folks came once the first year, and hid from sun in my bedroom, then spent this year erecting planks in their living room. Marking each sturdy post with numbers and arrows, a blueprint for the first house my sister and her husband will stand in.

My phone rings just as owls rustle onto my lone lemon tree. Moon-faced creatures with startling eyes that see sideways, they've nested outside my window. Dozing, peering, blinking until night, when they hunt. *Whoo, whoo,* they call as my phone trills on—I haven't set up a voice box either—and I imagine my father. Scarfed, pressing against wind that slows him down Lydig, where he walks daily to outrun his fate. I imagine the question he'll toss, the words I'll toss back. *If I come, where will I stay?*

ᔓ

My parents almost killed each other my storytelling night. To be less melodramatic, they crashed dishes into the sink. Ripped curtains off the racks. Flashed the very things they said belonged to low-class people: knives, scissors, broken glass. All the things I was supposed to stay away from because I was better than that. How were we royalty when we didn't even act middle-class? Or was this it, the fantabulous American Dream?

"Because of you," my father said, "she lost. You didn't practice with her. You let that other woman do your work."

"I'm on Zerega Avenue with you 24/7," my mother cried. "Should I cut myself in half? Take this! Cut me in half! Then everyone can have a piece!"

"Crazy," my father muttered. "Your family is crazy, you're crazy, and now she's turning crazy too. You spoil everything!"

"The only thing I spoiled was my life," my mother said, "the day I married you! And now she's turning out daughter-like-father! Spoiling my life again!"

I ran—out-out-out onto those faraway streets. Maybe, I thought, as I passed the synagogue, the hospital, the intersection where police lights swirled, I was a coward. I'd left my parents to that house, faces swollen red behind the rails, mouthing the words, *Nirmali, where are you going?* Maybe, I thought as I stalked the parkway flitting with leafy shadows, I was Manyara. I'd forsaken my family to find comfort in darkness, unguided. Or, I thought as I crossed the overpass of straggling cars, teenage boys on mini-bikes, I was Thumbelina. An anomaly from birth, doomed to roam without a people.

Whatever I was, I didn't know where I was going—until one familiar street, then another, and another, turned onto Zerega. Before the house my father built.

The full moon lit Zerega into a haunted mansion, something out of "The Tell-Tale Heart" by Poe, another Bronx storyteller who'd wandered these streets. This street too was dead, cars sugared and concrete frosted before black-icicled houses. I wondered if behind screen doors, children cried; if in shaded rooms, parents fucked in recompense; if families sat to dinner like ghosts, clamoring over marrow that was their own, licking wounds invisible to each other.

But I knew the secrets to just one house, so I crawled through the basement window I'd left ajar. The afternoon before this sudden snow, I'd been watching our Jamaican neighbors, a cellist and a trumpeter with a little boy and a littler girl always dressed in plaid, the picture of refinement sipping hot cocoa around their patio table. Centering the table was a pot of geraniums that bloomed blood all winter—*magic*, I thought as I tumbled through the window onto the dune-molded floor. But no magic in our deserted house—just the skeleton of drip-drop pipes along the peeling walls, and that nonchalant moon, wiggling its way up the whiny stairs to the done-and-redone living room.

Those mirror walls: silver, prismatic, perfect.

I was a shadow in all three walls, all nine panels.

Too perfect.

I couldn't bear the flashy beauty of this room, its obsession with image, how no matter where I turned, I couldn't hide from myself.

For Chrissake, mirrors were supposed to go on closet doors, walls were supposed to be bare. White. Plain. But no—*of course* my parents liked the gaudy look of money, *of course* they kept walls that might crash down and kill us, *of course* they wanted customers to notice not the patchwork house but their pristine reflection in it.

Well, that wasn't what *I* wanted.

My mother had left the toolbox by the entrance, and I picked out the wrench.

A heavy red thing, as long as my calf, with a serrated iron mouth, and when I swung it up like a bat, I was the goddess Kali the moment before the world ends.

SMASH—a spider grew across the right wall, first panel—CRUNCHCRUNCH—glass sprinkled down in huge triangles, jagged flakes—PING-SCREECH—I dragged lines across the unscarred mirrors—KAPOW—I banged into each wall, giving every panel its due, liberation from this prison.

And then—with glass falling like pieces from a puzzle, into my sweater, my scalp, my eyes that were no good—I sank into the middle of that empty room. I knew who I was. I was the ghost trapped in the other house, and even here among the glass, no one heard me. I sobbed like an animal, shrill at the moon. Then I wept in a low, soft tune punctuated by hiccups. At last, I went mute, simply waiting for dawn, rubbing the glass I'd loosened in sparkles on my skin, rubbing it all slowly in.

Sugar, Smoke, Song

SUGAR

After our Woodland spat, Yusuf disappears for three days. Anita, my South Indian roomie who dates nerdy Europeans, says, "Give it time. He's not a bad guy." Which is the phrase that got me back in Davis moping rather than in the Indian casino gambling.

Yusuf had stridden in as usual that afternoon, wearing his caramel leather jacket and plopping on our couch, but this time, he suggests driving through Woodland. When I ask why, he says, "Because it's finally raining. Because we always stay inside. Because you've never been, have you?"

First clue: he's smoking again, a habit he said he'd kicked, along with gambling and drinking and Zuleikha. But like a dope, I drive exactly where he wants me to. Up the county road, between sheep farms and olive groves, the hair on trees swishing down droplets, the sun flaming down ahead of us. I'm squinting so hard and driving by feel, while Yusuf goes on about how he used to drive up here almost daily.

"I'd be here all night sometimes, then go straight to work."

He's already on edge, dragging on the cigarette, but I ask, "I don't get it. What's the draw?"

He frowns at the sun. "The chance of beating the house."

"Wow," I say. "You *are* bad."

"*How*," he says, tossing the cigarette, "can you say that?"

"I meant, you've done some risky things."

Yusuf's voice crescendos. "Risky? Bad? Dangerous? You *know* that's what black men get called! I've never touched a joint to this day and I have to worry a hundred times more than coked up white boys about getting hounded by the cops."

I pull over by some ranch-style house on some winding side road and squeeze the wheel. "Please stop. You're scaring me. I hate arguing in the car."

Evil, he says, is when a regime locks up your father because he's a socialist. *Evil* is when you have to leave home at thirteen and learn that n—— is America's nickname for you. *Evil* is when you have to keep your voice down when your girlfriend's folks call or leave the apartment when they visit. Because you're not the same religion, you're not the right color.

I slap the dashboard and Yusuf jumps. "Stop talking to me like I'm some white girl. Don't *ever* pull that shit on me!"

I'm clicking open the door and he grabs my wrists. "Where the fuck do you think you're going?"

I hurl the keys at the backseat and say, "Go to hell or the casino or wherever the fuck you want with my car."

I sprint down the side alley, sobbing in Assamese: how I've ended up running down another strange road; how I haven't seen my folks in a year, haven't talked to my sister in four, and what does someone with a hundred siblings and aunts and uncles know about losing family; how I'm always the one who has to shut up and listen. I don't know if it's the slanting fence over some random lot of dead grass that catches me, but I lean over and feel how far I am from anything like home, despite all my maneuvers, all my bets. I stay angling like that toward the melting sun, the raucous birds, the in-evitability of nowhere-else-to-go until I'm breathing normally, my sniffling's stopped, and I begin to regret stranding Yusuf. As I walk slowly back, I think, *What if he's left with my car? What if something's happened to him? How will each of us get out?*

Yusuf is stalking back and forth before the car, yelling on the phone. I imagine it's Tariq because he's talking half in English, half in Amharic. "Yeah man, she just left me out here! In the middle of redneck Woodland!" When he sees me, he slams the phone shut and climbs into the driver's seat.

"Give me the keys." He extends his hand without glancing at me. "I would've left if I could've found them but you hid them real well right before you jumped."

I cover my face with my palms as I sob against the pane, and Yusuf glowers straight ahead as he drives the county road, tar against indigo sky.

Only when he pulls over at a gas station does he reach out his hand.

"I hate the silent treatment," I say. "I'm not gonna pay for shit if you don't talk!"

"So you gonna leave now?" he says. "You don't like it when I talk, you don't like it when I don't talk. Then you strand a brother in the middle of this racist-ass place. *Nobody* I know would pull a stunt like that. You know what it feels like for me to come out here?"

I slam the dashboard with both hands and Yusuf turns to stare. "You think I don't get called names? *Gook, sand n——*, or straight up *n——!* You know what *you* shouldn't have been doing? Yelling at me while I was driving! I *told* you that freaks me out!"

Yusuf slouches and I throw a twenty at him. "You're real good at fighting, aren't you?" he snarls, then steps out to pump gas, while passersby, mostly Mexican families, look worriedly at me massaging my forehead.

I'm remembering the first time Yusuf and I talked, not the club night he'd shown me his paintings on his flip but the weekend after, at Anita's birthday party. Yusuf had walked through the front door wearing a white shirt and a somber expression, as if showing his beautiful self were a difficult gift he were conferring on us all. The other guests, mostly tipsy scientists, stared as the most dazzling human being in the house followed me around. I too wondered, *Why?*

"It's nice to see you," I'd said.

He'd laughed. "So polite."

I handed him a plastic cup of pinot, then rushed to my private bath mirror. Hair un-frizzed? Check. Sarong straightened? Check. Eyeliner not blurred? Check.

When I inched back to the kitchen, Jasmine, a buxom punk rocker I'd met in voice class, was rattling off her number, the names of all her black friends, the list of painters she knew in Sac-town. Yusuf was studying her quizzically, cradling his cup in both hands, then turned to me, a grin popping out of nowhere. "You know what they say about Indian women?"

I braced myself by sitting on a barstool. "We are the hairiest?"

"They are the most beautiful in the world. Maybe I can paint you some time."

"I do nudes," Jas said.

"I won't hurt you," he said, taking my hand and brushing over the palm. "Looks like you've been through enough."

"I'm not afraid of paintbrushes," I said. "Or of you."

His hands were rough and dry, exactly the way I'd imagined a firefighter's hands to be, but cold. Just then, the house had churned, the partygoers scrambling out the door with their plastic cups, across the street, to the cleared-out parking lot. There, a safe distance from a few cars, Jas corralled two fire-breathers, one long-haired bearish Viking and A Girl with Some Kind of Tattoo lookalike. They'd dipped their sticks in a soda bottle of gasoline, then slipped them in their mouths, finally spewing columns of fire up into the placid Davis sky.

Tonight, it's only nine when Yusuf pulls us into my carport, the street bumping with Friday night hip-hop and punk rock, the asshole neighbors brawling because some dude hit on some other dude's wife. I wait in the seat, hoping for a miracle reconciliation, but Yusuf tosses my keys in the back, slams the door, and walks off down the driveway. I step numbly by the carport column and count the beats till his long line merges into the alley shadows, beyond the nodding gardenias and the neighbors' fenced-in noise.

SMOKE

Those first work mornings—farm furrows awash in light, crows lifting like a black veil from the trees, in hundred-degree heat that shimmers up the road, where folks walk in a perfect line—I feel, *maybe this is where I'm meant to be.* Truth is, so many of us have come here unannounced. My first learner this morning is a lanky Rwandan man with bloodshot eyes that seem like they've seen too much. It isn't until I've explained the rules, until I've taken down his Biography basics, until I've tested him with the first batch of words that I realize. He is my landlord's gardener, the man who has quietly repotted my dying alyssum, watered the parched soil so that the lone lemon tree stands fragrant and yellow.

"Are you that Tim?" I say.

His eyes gleam. "I am that Tim."

I pair him with an older white lady, a retired schoolteacher who has brought us sugar cookies. She stammers a bit in the beginning, as if she is the immigrant in a new country, and we may reject her application after all. Tim makes a few jokes about the heat to ease her and as they chew the cookies, I say what I always say. *Good luck, you will be fine, stay in touch.*

Over the summer, I find most of the learners have modest goals. Write a paragraph. Use the phone directory. Pay the bills. Some, who have left families behind in Rwanda or Cambodia or Mexico, want to write a letter. The grammar is off in various ways, but almost always, I read: *I miss you, I am doing something here, write me back.*

Every evening that I drive between Woodland and Davis, the flat of the valley seems even thirstier under the stark blue sky. The radio stations always talk about the drought, how the water table is at the lowest it's been in several years, how the valley is bursting into flame. I never call Yusuf, who will repeat how "fire is a demon, how water is a weapon. I never realized until I came to America." I want to call Deeta, to ask him a riddle like he'd ask me as a kid, *what did the farmer's son see in common between love and learning and land?*

At the interview for the job, the library ladies in their neutral blouses and dark sneakers had asked across the table, "Why do you care about this work? You could be making more back East. It says here, you want to work with singers." Impulsively, I said my grandparents hadn't been literate, that I was luckier than anyone in my family had been. When those ladies dropped *Iraq* and *unreadable* around me before they dropped me from the job, they must've concluded I was an uppity New Yorker anyway, but back then, they paused with their pencils perched on a checklist I never saw and turned away as if storing what I'd said for a rainy day.

Yusuf never asks about my work, though the night I began complaining about the words I bump against, he says, "Why are you doing these odd jobs for these crackers?"

"Are you saying I should leave town?"

"You take everything too literally and seriously."

"That's not what most people think. Plus I'm way funnier than you are."

He rolls his eyes and tells me to turn on the dresser light, show him whatever it is I wanted to show him. It's a New York Times article on soldiers in Somalia, and though he's narrated to me the differences of tone and tribe and war among Somalians, Ethiopians, and Kenyans, he's silent. He takes the laptop from me and clicks carefully through each picture. Lanky men in swaths of cotton, rifles slung over their shoulders, before fields of green-gold-black. "See," I begin, pointing to one byline. But Yusuf pushes aside my hand and mumbles, "A twenty-four-year-old . . . who trans . . . transports goods."

"Between borders," I whisper but Yusuf has clicked to the next page.

SONG

They say Cesaria would open her concerts by standing center stage, cigarette in one hand, glass of cognac in the other. Tick-tock five . . . ten . . . taking satisfied swigs of that cig, sipping ever so surely that pungent black liquor. As if this were some potent rite to open her cords, pump her belting breath, let the public know exactly what she were made of: not sugar and spice and all girls nice but sugar, smoke, song.

They say The Barefoot Diva of the orphanage sang on world stages—Lisbon, Paris, New York—as she'd sung in the Cabo Verde taverns and streets where she'd come up. Her voice never sounded harsh the way smokers' will, or languid the way drinkers' do, but deeply smooth, sweetly paced, even when singing about the untranslatable. *Morna, coladeira, funaná*: always those undertones of homesickness. The papers on her death mused how she never let the fame get to her but never questioned how she knew which was stage—which was sand, what is grand—what is shit, how scales other than pentatonic protect a bluesy heart.

SUGAR

And yet. The very next Friday, a sunny make-up Friday, Yusuf and I dress for Lake Berryessa. We're dawdling over folded prints at the bed's edge when he confesses: he fought again with Zuleikha.

"The way she yelled! 'How could I throw you in her face,' she said!"

"Why did you even call her? I feel like a dumb bitch."

"I thought we were friends," he says, rolling a white wifebeater on to match my tank. "I told her I was on a date."

"She acts like she has some claim on you. She's still in love with you!"

Yusuf turns away, ducking his bashful smile, but preens side-to-side before the bath mirror. "I'm a Greek god," he laughs, and winds toward me. I turn my back to him, so he can trace the birds tattooed down my spine, and wait for his firefighter's hands at the very bottom. They force in heat, pushing me down—he goes—and whispers, "Thatta girl. Stay right there."

Even my car, Yusuf eases round the crags to the lake, where my friends've warned me not to go. "Indian burial ground," they say. "Full of lost souls. Haven't you heard of the Zodiac Killer?" The way folks glance over as Yusuf and I clamber up the rocks, they must be conjuring: the squaw and the slave, here come The Browns, who's the twelve-year-old, who's her molester? Yusuf rolls his eyes but mocks the bearded Chicano who dusted me off when I stumbled onto shore: "Maria, Maria, whatchu doin' with that n——? Come to Papi."

Because I'd asked for this thistled hike, Yusuf riffs as he steers us round the motorboat fiesta dotting the longest stretch. "Yo, this is some bougie hippie shit. Look at the white boys owning the water. You sure you don't wanna be hanging with them? Why am I so nervous—you're just a little girl."

And yet. As I thread through seaweed and driftwood on the stretch's quieter end, Yusuf sloshes three yards behind, smoking a Marlboro Light. Black dogs, like so many pampered pooches in these boonies, bound toward me, and I trip over my sunken feet. As if I'd self-baptized, I rise soaked and zombie-walk on, toeing for shells or stones that might change my luck. Yusuf laughs—"Pa'lante! I like your attitude"—and scoops me up—"Put me down! I don't need your help!" I punch—but sand spills out my cutoffs and Yusuf laughs so hard he nearly keels us over. I can't help laughing back when he rolls us under an oak, its shadow merging with Yusuf's own, and shouts at the sun. "Look at how America's brought us to our knees! I used to live in a palace! God, give me a break! Give me a girl!"

"My ex," I say, "told me he was leaving me for a white girl. I'm not putting up with that colored boy psychosis anymore."

"You remind me," Yusuf says, "of my Eritrean girl. Small and fierce. She cheated on me with a brother."

When I tell him brothers don't notice me but old white men look at me like shank, Yusuf says, "Filet mignon. White boys'll give you five babies, then leave you for a supermodel."

"Brothers pull that shit too."

And yet. As flames fan and crackle over the valley's matchstick brush that August, I'm the one hunting for Yusuf. On an afternoon errand to downtown Sac, I park in the narrow lot of a Whole Foods and wander—half-breathing, half-hoping—to the back counter where he's said he works.

Sure enough, he's hamming in his green duds behind the sirloin and salmon, explaining prices to the white-swathed Ethiopian women with a cart. I know he sees me because he tries too hard not to look sideways. As the ladies discuss prices with each other, I walk up. "Do you have any fish?"

He grins. "I'll keep something in the back for you."

"I thought you might be gallivanting."

"No fancy words here. And no lying."

The ladies are assessing us now and when I begin backing off, he says, "Where are you going so soon?"

Truth is, I'm shy suddenly and burning with the possible read of *jealous girlfriend*, which I never thought I'd stoop to being. Truth is too, I want to watch Yusuf undetected, so I lurk about the grocery like a shoplifter. Browsing aisles of canned beans, Mexican spices, dairy I can't digest. He cuts statuesque even as he's grumpily winding back and forth from the meats to the freezer door. I look up at myself in the monitor: scarved in a black puffy jacket, small, bookish. A year later, when I see Yusuf's new girl, an Ethiopian woman built like me but who works alongside him, I won't wonder as I do now what he wants and what he doesn't.

But the most surprising truth I don't learn until my tutoring gig resumes and Yusuf's tackling night classes again: *history will Braille right under you.* Davis is chilling into California Winter—no telltale snow—still Yusuf, insisting *all work and no play makes Yusuf a dull boy,* steers my car to the downtown Czech pub where we met. It's there, as we cross the wood gate, just two yards between them, that Yusuf and some barstool blonde swivel toward each other—it's then I feel the frisson in their fists, I see their daggers of love. Yusuf slinks like a cowed dog round the column, she lifts her arched brows, her lovely lashes like a proud flag, and I march into the reggae that throbs from the turntable-styled bar. "I'm Nirmali," I say, and the way she grips my hand, announces "Zuleikha," I know she's the tougher bird.

She is, about-facing and bobbing off into the crowd, while Yusuf drinks Corona after Corona and I jab the mint in my rum.

"You look unhappy," he says. "Let's just go."

"Did you know she'd be here?"

"I swear I forgot."

"I don't want to be some pawn in whatever's going on between you two."

"You have no idea! I haven't even held that girl's hand in a year."

Yet he rises twice, fifteen minutes, then twenty, to smoke on the porch where she sits, blowing steam up, steadily ignoring him.

She isn't beautiful, just a girl who knows the price of her booty and blonde, whereas strangers stop to tell me I'm a gem, and tonight, I almost believe it. Yusuf's painter fingers slipped purple silk on my bronze skin, feathers between my black curls, glossed my eyes into emerald wings. Yet, this is precisely how I recognize their love: I am the showpiece he brings in order to sit at her table.

Later, in the blunt light of my sparse room, my dress crushed over his jeans, my thighs pried apart like a clam, he murmurs,

"Such beautiful, beautiful legs." I know it's my ear his tongue licks but I wonder which bird he craves. When I ask him how he likes it, he flips me and runs a hand past the scars circling my hips. "Good," he says. "Very good."

SMOKE

Every month we Skype, Deeta forgets to adjust the computer screen. All we see of his low head are owl eyes searching. Ma, who perches at the screen's side, who pats her molting hair, listens for the *love* I won't utter before gliding away. Every month we count, on both hands, Deeta's procedures and Ma's shots. Three angioplasties, one triple bypass, a couple stents. Morning insulin, midnight snacks, Ma shaking as she slices a banana in the kitchen. *Criminal Minds*, a habit Ma and I still share, flickers on Anita's television behind each screen chat, stalling me in wakefulness I can never leave behind.

When I call Henna to bridge the years, she says, "Ma will have to retire soon. What will she do if Deeta dies? An old Asian immigrant woman with ten years of savings?"

Suddenly I can't remember Henna's numbers: promises, promotions, absences. "I'm not planning to run out on anyone," I say.

"Do *you* have any savings?" she says. "I can't raise kids *and* take care of them."

I stare at my chapped hands, unsure if I'm more ashamed of myself or her.

"Don't tell me another story, Nirmali," she says and hangs up.

My first visit back to the Bronx in a year, right before Yusuf jostled me on African Night at Little Prague, Deeta drives Ma and me to Orchard Beach. A gray June day, so the lot is nearly empty, save for the ginormous white tent by the exit road. *Harlem All State Circus*, the letters painted on the side read, and Deeta, who likes to repeat names aloud, says, "Harlem! In the Bronx!" Ma squints at the tent, at the beach, then stares at the sky.

They pace forward without me, their parallel powerwalk along the boardwalk, at a careful distance from the still warm Atlantic tide. I plop myself at the edge of the curb, between the courtside fence and the parking lot, which is when the acrobat and his little buddy bike by. He looks surprisingly like Yusuf, with a lion's crown of twisties, those large lashed eyes, and that limber grace.

"What are you doing here all by yourself?" he says.

"I wish I knew."

He bikes before me in circles, grinning, and his seven- or eight-year-old friend trots after him tirelessly.

"I'm an acrobat at the circus. You know what that is?" Acrobat Man drops his bike, cascades backward toward the cars in a series of handstands and somersaults and cartwheels. He does the whole tumbling dance back my way, panting not a bit as he lands on one knee before me.

"How about it? Two free tickets for the pretty lady? Come on Saturday," and he gives me two slips of paper.

"I don't know . . ." but he is already biking back to the tent, lifting a hand without glancing back. His little copycat waves too, his back halfway turned, still peeking.

When Ma and Deeta steer the car out the lot, I hunch unbelted behind Deeta's seat and say, "Did you forget about me or something? I thought I'd never find you."

They don't answer—Ma gazing stony-faced at the sea, Deeta coughing and clenching the wheel—but as we pass the blue-and-white tent, I say, "I got invited to the circus."

"Really?" Deeta says genially. "You should go."

"Who," I say, "would I know there?"

"It might be fun," Ma says. "Maybe you will meet someone."

"What if they ask me to join?"

Ma laughs. "Is that any different from what you do now?"

SONG

They say Edith Piaf was raised in the streets, and the streets rushed into her that sound. Boisterous, salt-of-the-earth, unapologetically *Padam!* in a tiny thing they called The Sparrow. They say, when she made it to America, audiences hated her black dresses, her somber expressions, her incomprehensible French. But her undisguised pain, they say, was why so many Others adored Piaf, what gave her that bust-the-roof power and that power its *c'est la vie* face to those who could sing high-and-hard with her.

They say the love of her life was a married boxer who, after instant-dying in a car crash, knocked her heart out so thoroughly she had to stuff the hole with morphine, with drink. They say the Church wouldn't dignify her with a funeral mass, though her dead voice called forth *100,000* onto Paris streets. They say the long echo of her was her drama, on and off the stage, so operatic of course she wielded a voice that, her father the circus man said, "could drown out the lions."

SUGAR

In the beginning, Yusuf would tell me stories of the back-ruining work digging trenches, quenching fires that had sprung up all over the county in a deepening drought. He would set me on his lap and say calmly, those chapped hands turning my face this way and that in the sun, "Where else would someone like you have met someone like me, Nirmali, except at a party?"

"We're not *that* different."

"Never forget, you are not black."

"You know what was the first word that came to me when I saw you? Unhinged."

He shooed me off his leg and said scornfully as he yanked open the back screen door, "You're beautiful, Nirmali, but you're weird."

"I could say the same of you," I shouted but he would have closed the glass door, so that I'd have to walk round and ring my own front bell.

In the first month, I learned Yusuf knew a million things about the Shoah, about the poetry and protest after Nakba, though we'd argue about whether Indians were Arab or Asian. "I've seen the Middle East," he said one night, before a daylong TV series on Bob Marley's live concerts. "They have your color, your features, your food."

"The rest of my family gets mistaken for Korean or Filipino or Mexican," I said, thinking back to guessing games in the Bronx, over some grocery register or before a subway map placard. "It's not that simple for us." But he'd turned away, clicking up the volume on the remote. "Whatever you do, don't make me eat any more couscous or watch any more genocide documentaries. I'm done."

When mid-summer heat gave way to late summer fires, I learned Yusuf could only talk about love in code. There was the night he came bearing Robin Williams' *What Dreams May Come*, a movie even sappier than a Bollywood flick. He lounged on the futon, holding me so tightly I couldn't breathe, while he paused on every painting-heaven scene.

"Can you believe this kind of love?"

No, I can't.

There was the night he came with *Coming to America*, Yusuf rewind-replaying the moment Eddie Murphy, discovering his chosen bride is, in fact, his American love, beams, his whole suited self glowing with this new meaning to marriage. "Isn't it funny?" Yusuf said. "Like he's gotten a Christmas present."

Then there was the night he brought *V for Vendetta* and said, slipping the disc into my laptop, "It's a smarty-pants movie." He warned me he might fall asleep halfway through, and when I said what's the point of watching alone, he said he wasn't going anywhere, and curled against me as he snored.

Then there was the night he came fragrant with beer, jittery in his buttercream leather jacket. "You're late," I said, rubbing my hand along the arms and tiptoeing for his lush lips. "I love this jacket."

"It's from Tariq." He walked off to my bedroom. "That guy loves me like a brother."

He lay halfway on the bed, an open Corona bottle in hand, his legs planted on the gray carpet. I sat near him, my hands rising-falling on his chest, and he said he's been to see his folks. "My brother said, 'Yo Yusuf, what's going on, you still seeing that nice Indian girl?'"

"They don't remember my name?"

"I'm almost thirty. I'm a grown man with no time to waste. Do you understand what I'm saying?"

"You've told me this."

"I spent two years with a woman who hid me from her folks, who was going on blind dates while we were still living together."

I lay my hands on my lap and wondered what burned more: Yusuf hung up on Zuleikha, Yusuf withstanding more for her than he would for me, myself the one nursing his wounds.

"I welcome you into my home. I'm still waiting for you to get checked. I've told my folks about you"—I didn't mention Yusuf sweating beside me that afternoon—"how many of these have you done?"

"Okay, okay," he said, sandwiching my hands between his. "I'm just talking aloud is all."

Which sounds untrue, I wanted to shout, *to someone who teaches singing and reading,* but I fibbed too. "Whatever. It's up to you."

Still holding my hands, he looked away, said nothing at all.

Years later, when I'm counting the red flags on the one Indian man I've ever dated, a toothy journalist who approached by asking why everyone knew about Syria but not about Kashmir, who it turned out was still pining over his Ethiopian ex on the nights he stewed red lentils alone, I'll wonder about triangles. How old they are, what they leave out, why two sides always, even minutely, overshadow the third.

It's no different on my August visit home, hoping to trade a blistering sky for a little childhood rain. Ma and Deeta shuffle in their kitchen like worn mahouts offering pithas, tangy fish, curry goat to a mad elephant. This no-sound ritual, even with Uncle and Auntie there, means licking my knuckles and listening to love tonics from Assam, Mumbai, the Islands.

"Zuleikha tried to seduce Yusuf," Auntie says, "though she was married to another man."

"Christians cheat too," Deeta says but Auntie doesn't flinch.

"When Yusuf scorned her, she had him jailed," she says. "Later, Yusuf, free and rich, finds Zuleikha, an old widow, on the street, and because she still loves him, he marries her."

"Romantic," Uncle says. "But a bit fairy-taleish, no?"

"A fantasy," Ma laughs. "Men want dogs."

"So do women," Auntie says. "That's why I tell our girls: friendship first."

What do I listen to but Yusuf's pause when I tell him I miss him, right at midnight, car alarms blaring down empty streets, teens jeering bittersweet nothings from stoops.

"Nirmali, you can't buy family in the store." I start to snort *why* but he ends, "I'll call you tomorrow."

He doesn't and I'm left stringing words for ten nights like nonsense ads on train rides to and from the city: *Dios Cristo, seduce scorn. Only when free and rich. Knuckle loved, cheat married, fairytale darkly. Bendiga salva! Tomorrow luv. Tomorrow tomorrow tomorrow.*

But tomorrow flies me to September nights so smoky I can barely breathe and to Yusuf, who tosses about in my bed, never his. He will sweat over some painting he hasn't made, for a man he hasn't seen since thirteen and, covering his eyes with an elbow, will say, "I'm going to start a fraternity. Boys without fathers not allowed."

"Plenty of great guys don't have dads."

"My sister mailed me his stopwatch. I take it out of the drawer to hold, but I can't wear it."

"At least your sister mails you," I will say but Yusuf will move on to Zuleikha. How she dated Arab men while they lay like man and wife. How she muffled his mouth when her mother called, and evicted him when her father visited.

When I yank the cover over my head and mutter "lovesickness," Yusuf will move on to his Eritrean girl. How she lied about sleeping with a friend of a friend. How he'd dumped her, this girl he should've married. How he couldn't, when she fled to San Jose, track her down.

When I jab on the desklight, Yusuf will roll away, bare back an impossible wall.

"You're Lear and I'm Cordelia," I will say, hugging my knees.

"Once again no one knows what you're talking about."

"Before Lear divides his kingdom, he asks which daughter loves him the most. The first two compare him to the sun and moon, even to their husbands, but the last says he's salt. Furious, Lear casts Cordelia out, though she's the one who takes him back when he's lost everything."

I will sink my fingers into Yusuf's hair but his temples will rise and fall in dreams we do and do not share, of families we may never find again: *without you, love, nothing tastes the same.*

Smoke

The mid-year evaluations come in spurts. Some pairs have hit the ground running, others have hit sudden bumps, and still others have not once touched base. *Catalogs of life,* I think, as I make the drive down the light-blanketed county road to the Woodland office.

Beulah, my Woodland boss, insists, each time my car or bike has broken down on this or that road, "You have to show up." She is a pinched-looking blonde with frog eyes made more amphibian by her glasses, and every mini-crisis in the Literacy calendar makes her twirl-tug her curls so tightly it seems she might tweeze herself bald. But if there's anything I've learned from her antsy rules, her antsy reviews, it's *show up and you will be surprised.*

Today, she spreads out the reports like a puzzle between us, the top three files the learners whose paths have taken the most surprising turn: Srey, Tim, and José. Srey, the one with the older white husband, has disappeared altogether; Tim and his volunteer were racing along but have hit some scheduling snags; and José, who for so long would sometimes show, sometimes not, is on the verge of taking his citizenship test.

"I don't understand what happened," she says, almost cheerily, as if this were the find of the week. "I really thought Srey's husband was going to keep her on track. And look—our dark horse wins the race."

I stare at the files, trying not to make some feather-ruffling joke about how people of color are not animals to be gambled on. So I put my left hand on Srey's top paper, only half checkmarked, and say, "I think her husband couldn't drive her around anymore because of work. He didn't want her taking the bus by herself."

"Ah, so protective," Beulah smiles. "Young love!"

Rather than point out Srey's husband is at least twice her age, I put my right hand on Tim's last written report, where he spoke about wanting to write a memoir about the Rwandan genocide, and say, "Mrs. Janowski dropped out. She says she loved working with Tim but just can't commit the time anymore."

Beulah purses her lips and frowns at me. "None of us can expect too much from the seniors. Besides, her son and grandkids are visiting and she never gets to see them!"

Perhaps I deserve the schoolmarm scolding because I'm thinking, *Well, half Tim's family was wiped out, so he doesn't have a choice.* But I can't help liking Mrs. Janowski, who cheered on Tim for every book finished, who wrote pages and pages of how much she'd herself learned, who is one of the few folks around here about to vote for Obama rather than McCain.

The afternoon light is pouring in through the upper windows of the back room, where the library also holds Anonymous meetings, services for prisoners, potlucks for young moms and their kiddos. Everything inside the room seems afire: racks of books to be shelved in the corner, stuffed bears lined along the radiator under the windows, walls of posters citing meeting dates, *Lord let me know what I can change.*

I pick up José's application with his initial goals sheet in both hands, and Beulah softens before me. "He did it," she says. "Make sure you send him a rulebook right away of the citizenship test."

"He's been through three different volunteers," I say, tracing with a finger the timeline of his stops and starts a year ago, when I started the job. "He didn't give up."

Beulah snaps back to cheery mode. "Better late than never!"

Which is the point that haunts me a month later, when she and another white lady take me into a room without windows, explaining that I am to be let go because I'm late too often, I'm hostile, I'm timid, I'm unprofessional, I'm not adjusted to the local demographic. Neither brings up the previous week, when I'd called Beulah out for leaving the Storytime kids unsupervised with a volunteer who had a record, a blonde lady who came up later to say, "That was when I was young and dumb," and I told Beulah, "The rules are the same for everyone." For an hour, I will struggle to breathe lower and speak louder: *I had been late because of transportation issues, my time wasn't free yet I'd been asked to pick up work after hours, one can't be timid and hostile at once, unprofessional means this interrogation, the targets of war are a demographic too.*

But her words will outweigh mine, so that my girls will again ring me. Jas will say, *What else is new, sweetie? Women tearing each other apart? And you know, you do take your time.* Anita will say, *You're overqualified anyway, Mali. It's fine to do public service but what about your voice work? You wouldn't have gotten anywhere with them.* Rosie will say, *You made those white girls look bad and then you got uppity about it. Those hicks went easy firing you rather than shooting you.* Yusuf will be long gone by then but I imagine him repeating what he'd said when he'd picked me up once from the branch. "For someone so smart," he said, shaking his head, "you can be so naïve."

Song

They say The Nightingale of Bollywood, Lata Mangeshkar, lost her father young, a tragedy that pushed her, the oldest, to singing for studios, to growing into Lata of the sari-bindhi, Lata of the *aye mere watan ki logon*, Lata of more songs than any recorded artist in history—excerpt perhaps her sister.

LataLataLata, who crossed genres the way desis crossed oceans, bidden and everywhere, her tones warming our workdays, our family functions, our outsider nights. *Ajeeb dastan hein yeh / This is an unusual tale*: a nurse in her white, widow-like sari serenades her doctor love, as he glooms beside his swanky wife beside the improbable palms. *Yara seeli seeli / Friend, slowly slowly*: a ghost haunts the shorn-tree sands and her skeptic friend, Samir, born again to fulfill his promise to jailbreak her from a king's lust. *Pyar kiya toh darna kya / When one has loved, what's to fear*: a slave girl declares her love for another Samir, spinning before his furious father, King Akbar, who, it's said, had also romanced her, who, it's shown, would entomb her alive.

What I want to know is, how do you sing in words you can't speak, feelings you may not know? After India lost to China in '62, after Nehru forsook the Assamese to the Chinese, was she crooning *loss* and *blood* for him, for mainlanders, or for us? When you *have* felt words in ways you're warned you can't say, how do you guard any sweetness of heart, any saltiness of voice, from sisters-haters-businessmen-ideologues that want to eat you, then spit you back out?

Sugar

Like another Halloween ghoul, Yusuf begins wandering in midnights, no sex between us, just the smell of beer he's drunk with friends I've never met, and tales I wish I couldn't read. How he went to some strip club with his boys, how he danced with some girls at a bar, how he fought with Zuleikha again for an hour. *Love, love, love,* he's taunting me, *don't you wish you had some of mine?*

"I don't care if you dance with other girls. You know why? Because I *choose* to trust you. Why don't you just go back to Zuleikha?"

"I don't know if I can handle you," he says, looking weirdly pleased. "Why do you stay with me?"

I frame his long face between my hands. "You remind me of home."

Thing is, even at red lights, when Yusuf brakes my car, when white girls roll down their windows and holler, Yusuf looks steadfastly at the road, though I can see his back, always tight and forward, as if protecting himself. They are tall blondes like Zuleikha, which makes me nervous and touched, and I find myself leaning out my own window, like a startled bird ready to flee.

My girls offer different reads that say more about them than Yusuf or me. Jas says over rum and coke, "So has his hose put out your fires yet?" Her hair is newly streaked blue and green and all the white rocker boys in their ripped jeans are eyeing her zaftig orbs, but she chuckles. "Why're you holding back? If you don't want him, give him to me! I'll wear him out!"

Anita, whose cousins sell cosmetics in East Africa, says, "There are two things you have to understand, Mali. He's like a traditional Indian man, which is why he looks at you confused. Also, colonialism wrecked Africa, down to their family structure. He's one of hundreds of lost boys, so don't take what he's doing as a reflection on you."

Rosie, the African American tutor I met through one of the learners, says after the Woodland fight, "How interesting. He talks to you like you're a black girl." She's been debating whether she wants to have babies with her husband, a good Philly Muslim who'd like to raise kids in the faith. "I'm not gonna raise them with two stigmas!" She presses a warm finger between my eyebrows. "Loving one of us, Nirmali, is no joke. Black men might be the most insecure in the world but there's also no love like ours."

By November, Yusuf has committed to school full-time, and when he comes, he is too worn for talk though not for sex. Nights together are getting briefer, rougher, so that one night, as Yusuf is going at it, I tell myself, *maybe this will get less painful, maybe it's a matter of time, maybe like Yusuf's mantra about trust it's like learning a fine wine.* But the night Yusuf enters in the wrong place, though I've asked him not to, I finally speak. I shake him up at 3:00 a.m., when I'm sleepless again, and he rises startled, as if I'm the ghost.

"I don't want to do that anymore," I say. "You hurt me. Last time, I bled from the back for days."

"Nirmali," he says, rubbing his forehead. "Maybe we aren't sexually compatible. Maybe we should just end things here."

"What are you talking about?" I say. "Just because I'm telling you one thing I don't like doesn't mean you throw the whole thing away!"

He sits on the edge of my bed, his back turned to me. "You don't want me here. You're going to tell people I pushed you."

I place both palms on his back, as if they are heart clamps that might resuscitate this. "I never said those things. I'm saying, this needs to feel good for me too. But I'm in pain. Are you listening to me at all?"

He turns his face to me, a strangely guarded look hooding his eyes. "This is getting too hard. I'm waiting and waiting for you to open up, to give yourself to me. I'm not going to waste another two years!"

"Everything takes time," I say, clasping his palms between mine in prayer pose. "Please. We'll talk about this in the morning, when you're not tired."

He sighs and rolls away to the wall, and we never speak of it again.

After Yusuf and I stop sleeping together, my girls write their own conclusions. Jas cries, tears on my neck as she hugs me. "It's okay, Mali. Just call it what it was. Use the word." Anita scrunches her face and hugs herself, as if she cannot believe this had happened in the house where we'd welcomed him. "Unbelievable! So selfish! Just like an Indian man!" Rosie, for this reason or another more important to her, stops returning my calls at all.

Just like that, as if the fires had sapped any energy left, lights go out all over town. I flick on every switch in the house, the hallway—*no*—the kitchen—*no*—my bedroom—*no*—then sit on the couch, feeling the shadows of every object about me. Anita will not be back from the lab till night, lost these days in a little molecule called nitric oxide, "so diminutive but needed for life," she says. "Without it," she grins while spearing a sausage, "we die." But I cannot even call Anita, and when I scrape up a lighter flame and hold it to my busted phone bottom, where the batteries crowd, the bottom begins to melt, like the black ice seeping from my chest to fingers and toes: the ice of disappeared boyfriends, the ice of my once-upon-a-time sister, the ice of friends and family tightroping their own darkness.

I drive from memory to Yusuf's place, where I've dropped him when his car's been stopped up. (A car, he likes to remind me, his Palestinian girl got for him.) But his block is also blacked out, only a few stragglers looking curiously at me as I walk up to the gate, peer through its bars at the row houses.

"Are you looking for someone?" a Spanish-sounding man says, stepping back from unlocking his door.

I wonder if this man, peering back at me half-puzzled, half-wryly, knows more of the story than I do. *Yo hombre*, he'll say, *your side chick came checking in on you.* "Thought I had a friend who used to live here," I say, walking backward across the street.

The highway out of Sacramento, past creviced fields that, by day, look like golden vaults flooded with water, is an ominous ribbon of shawled land. So I find myself driving by memory into Davis, to where the Krishnans live, in a small apartment by the co-op at the edge of town.

Mrs. Krishnan's face twists into surprised amusement as she opens the door, perhaps upon seeing my distressed face, my intertwined hands. "Nirmali," she laughs, and her husband, her doe-eyed seven-year-old, her gentle-faced brother-in-law and his Rapunzel-haired singer wife crowd the door. Mrs. Krishnan has candles lit all over the ground floor of the apartment, dark red and orange-yellow candles that cast swimming flecks of boxes and ovals on everything. We sit at their long table, where I've had tea several times with Anita for her Malayali dance practices and maybe I'm really waiting for her to return, because I'm tensing myself through dinner platitudes. The Indian husbands with their lashed looks of concern are telling me to never tell my Indian husband, when I find a good one, that I've had other boyfriends; to tell him he is my very, very first. *They look happy,* I think of each couple, the little girl, in frills and pigtails, as elated as a ripe balloon between them. *I want this circle, I want this yogurt with chili seeds crushed in it, I want this high-ceilinged house of candles even in the city-wide dark. But,* I think half-spooning rice and dal into my mouth, *I've never been good at lying, even if it could've saved my ass.*

Anita raps on the window, then sighs heavily at the door, as if she'd been looking all over town for a naughty cat. "I thought I'd find you here," she smirks, as if really, were it not for my silliness, we would've been chugging a beer in our dark house. The talk resumes its easy rhythm, though faster now, slipping into Malayali I can't follow, but I guess at the same thread when Anita's face takes on that odd, hardened look.

"Forget all this," she tells me in the car, the town lighting awake house by house, the bikers circling bravely with their lone red lamps. "They're old school."

"Maybe I am too."

"Nirmali, whatever you do, don't write him. He's gone."

SMOKE

Tim, the learner who is also my landlady's gardener, comes around like clockwork, twice a week, before either Anita or I rise. More and more since his tutor has left, he lingers by the sliding glass, to see who it is I am, behind what I do. He is tall but hunched, as if permanently lost in thought, those lustrous eyes always streaked red. Like so many of the Africans I've met in Davis, he extends his hands in greeting, in reassurance. Today, he brushes the dirt off and clasps my hand while I perch uncertainly on the threshold of the garden. He wants to know what Yusuf used to try to figure out: where is my family, what is my background, what am I, a twenty-nine-year-old woman, planning to do here?

"Other than work, you mean?" I say.

"Work is not life. Wish I could do something other than this," he says. "How do you like our landlady?"

"She's difficult but fair."

"Yes, yes, exactly. I work with her now sixteen years." He taps his head. "A little crazy. After her father died, she went crazy. It's hard, you know, to lose your whole family."

He steps closer and peers behind me, as if to see if anyone's listening.

"Anyone, especially for boy, losing family, losing father . . . cannot be sane." I don't think he means just the landlady, and he takes my hand again. "Such a pretty, nice woman. We should talk somewhere else. Maybe over coffee."

I am tired suddenly—*I woke too early*—but say "Sometime. I'm so busy these days."

I don't see Tim again until The Learners' Celebration two weeks later, when I've lost so much weight from stress, he walks by me. Despite the dismissal, I am slated for two more weeks of *wrapping up* projects, having to smile for the patrons, having to stretch dollars till I can pick up sub work at the other branches. But handing out certificates in the back verandah of the Sacramento Capitol, all marble and windows, is not the best part; or Beulah's scowl when the learners seem more eager to thank me than her; or meeting writers face-to-face whom I've known only in reports, like Anand from Fiji or Martin from Winters. It's listening to them read their essays aloud, while I sit behind a bouquet-laden table of pink-and-purple carnations.

How I Crossed a Desert, José reads to the hall of made-up families sitting tentatively at far-spaced tables. *My Second Life*, Martin reads as afternoon sun cascades to the hall's ends, Minerva plaques guarding every other door. *Words I've Lost*, Anand reads as folks scrape back chairs, plod to a center table of sandwiches, stubborn jaws relaxing. I crouch in my corner, listening to faltering tones not at all like the voice work I trained for, goosebumpy from these backshelf stories I've helped spill.

But when I fly to the Bronx Thanksgiving weekend, I have no story I want to admit. Ma and Deeta have been waiting an hour in the La Guardia arrivals terminal, and though they say little, their faces flush with a kid's joy and they play Bhupen Hazarika on the ride home. *O moina ketiya ahili toi, o little girl, when did you come?*

Each visit, Deeta gets skinnier, Ma heavier, so they walk this evening and every other through the Mideast sections of the Bronx. Deeta marches like a one-armed soldier, left side swinging-chopping, while Ma trips after him, trying to narrate a story to its punch line, joking to me that Deeta sometimes leaves her completely behind. I don't know why our file drives me crazy but I stop in the middle of Gunhill Road.

"If you're not gonna care whether we're behind you or not, then what's the point?"

"What's the point of what?" Deeta says.

"Exactly," I say, my voice rising so that the Salvadoreans kicking a soccer ball on the parkway pause to stare. I can feel myself morphing into sixteen-year-old Mali again. Fists clenched on these streets, stalking-stalking through sweat or snow.

Deeta slumps, looking smaller than I'd imagined he could, halfway between the boulders and the bodegas and the pine tree-shaded houses. "Please. Let's walk together. As a family."

Ma doesn't say anything, just looks off at the projects where she works, as if she might see someone she knows. All I can see is how we're hovering apart like tilted dominoes, never coming together like on those boards the old island men slap together Sundays at the park.

"I can't keep up with you two. I'll wait at home. You enjoy yourselves."

My last midnight home, Ma shuffles from the kitchen to the sofa, where I'm chewing turkey strands before *Criminal Minds*, and munches a long while on a saltine. "Twenty years," she says finally as the black cop captures the one white psychopath, a victory not at all like life outside the house. "Twenty years at home without money is not a small thing, Mali-ma." She untangles my back hair nest, and I hear her telling me, it's not shameful to say no, maybe it's okay to come home, that my body is her body is our body that, no matter where I run, will always equal one.

SONG

They say Philomela wove a tapestry to tell her sister how Tereus, her sister's husband, had raped her. Tereus the royal—which equaled, even then, undue admiration and impunity—had seen something he liked and grabbed it. Who cared about ancient laws or one woman's insistent *please, nos*? Turns out, Tereus cared after Philomela wove her truth-telling tapestry, and outed his selfish jerk, rich boy ass to the public. He cared after Procne, his wife, fed him his son in stewed cutlets, and voila! when it was boykind, he saw the blood on his hands. But because some corner of him needed affirmation he wasn't *a monster*—and because blame, like energy, must *go* somewhere after the event—Tereus cut off Philomela's tongue.

The goddesses of girls took pity on Philomela crawling, Philomela bleeding, Philomela slurring. They hovered in a circle about girlkind's first whistleblower, and said, *for the price you have paid for your tapestry-truth, we transform you.* Philomela's long limbs thinned and sprouted into feathered wings, her aching bones and sluicing organs became a bird's reedy innards, and up-fzzz she whirred, to the steady hand of a pine. A nightingale, her classical trills and plaintive power a warning to girls in their most incorrigible parts.

(Correction: in real life, the female cannot sing.)

SUGAR, SMOKE, SONG

My last Yusuf sighting, I'm riding the midday bus for a last-minute shift at the Woodland library. Two–three months after his New Year's text, after he's left me with credit card charges, after he's stopped responding to questions at all. Two–three days after my car engine has smoked up again on the freeway, so that I sit on one of two lone buses bumping past razed fields, my sunglasses on against the sun. Yusuf appears as suddenly as he had at Anita's party: hair grown back, twisties up in that mane I'd asked him to keep, and I can't help wondering, for whom has he resurrected the Firefighter Lost Boy?

I hear myself dialing Ma, mumbling in Assamese as Yusuf slumps across me, staring at my knees as if they're a still life Cézanne, looking thinner, wearier than I've ever seen him. We face off like that, me not remembering what I say to Ma, who asks again and again if I'm busy, Yusuf's gaze boring through my shades, that dusty aisle between us and all the empty seats.

When the bus pulls up into the Woodland Mall parking lot, I

curl in my corner till even the driver shuffles off. It hits me then—lingering behind the seniors at the connecting stand, the seniors boarding the 1:00 p.m. bus for the casino—where Yusuf's going. He won't let me see the proof however, and walks away from the casino bus, head up, shoulders squared, into the vast lot. I tense, sweaty-palmed on the bench, with clarity—knowing neither he nor I have any business lingering in this town.

No way I could have predicted this detour at Christmas, when Yusuf had taken me to a friend's wedding. The air around us flammable, my greetings salty from a visit home, and still Yusuf decided to introduce me to his family. Though he neglected to say so until I sat paralyzed before his three brothers and two sisters at an Oakland wedding table. "Why're you so quiet?" they asked before rising. They paraded through the piano hall like they were the real music—women in embroidered white linen, men in pressed blue suits—and I was the dissonant note, shuffling in a gold sari Yusuf suggested I wear.

"Don't abandon me," I whispered and Yusuf steered me to the dance circle, where he nestled me between his sisters, then disappeared. The girls were kinder than I expected, the freckled one nudging my shoulders into an Arab shake, the rosewood beauty holding my ashol gently, but I strained for Yusuf's roar. When I caught it through the window, I stumbled with my Johnnie Walker into the dark, where Yusuf and his brothers puffed their stories at the sky.

"They shot that n—— right in front of the house," the youngest said, measuring my face. "I thought about calling, but who gives a fuck about a black man in Oakland?"

"Did he die?" Yusuf asked.

"Hell yeah," his brother said.

I didn't say what I was thinking—*strange decision*—just nodded. "The price of a black man's life."

"So you an artist too," the skeptical-faced one said.

"Art-lover," I said. "I'd like to teach voice but I'm working in literacy right now."

He looked at Yusuf like *told you so* rolled into the cig he dragged, but said, "Good for you. I'm Tariq. Maybe Yusuf told you, we grew up together."

Inexplicably, Yusuf shaded his eyes and mine, then yanked us inside, where a singing crowd bobbed up on two chairs the slender Ethiopian groom and his muscled blonde wife. *May your love last as long as Abraham and Rebekah's,* the hoarse voices cheered. The hall vibrated with their chorus—*jubilee* I thought—but when I said, "I trust you now," Yusuf turned to the men sliding from hall-end to end. They were clapping long sticks and shoulder-shaking one another on, and when Yusuf, anchored to my hand, leaned in with his own stick, the old ladies fixed their dewy eyes on me. The way they'd cradled his cheeks when he'd made the rounds earlier, he had a hundred mothers for the one vigil-ing by his dad. But like a boy who wants something so badly he doesn't care how, Yusuf let the stick clatter on a table to finger my bangled wrists, my stray curls. And just that brashly, we spun each other in the hall until the music rolled us, drunk on tej, out onto the speckled streets and sky, and just that smoothly, Tariq drove us, blasting Tupac and JLo over my fretful nap, to that Davis house one last time. It's only then, by my bed, Yusuf unwinding my sari, that I blurted, "Those ladies . . . " but he cut in, "Tomorrow, they'll all be talking."

New Year's Eve, when I finally show Ma the wedding pics, she snorts. Me and Yusuf at the dinner table, me and Yusuf in a group photo, me and Yusuf alone by Tariq's car. I thought he'd looked handsome in his deep blue shirt and say so, but Ma frowns. "Why do you always have a drink before you?" She is upping her insulin dose, injecting herself in the darkest corner of her bedroom, by the altar of gods. Where once she'd been an abalone-shelled pixie, her stomach has swollen into a bruised pouch. She eats the one roti, the turmeric cabbage, with her head bowed, as if a continent only she knows of is growing in her belly, draining her.

When Ma accuses me again of being the reason Deeta is sick, and Deeta takes me sobbing to Orchard Beach so we can talk about Yusuf, I tell him, "He's the closest thing I've got to you." When Deeta tells Ma, "We didn't raise them to think like this, not here," Ma says to me on a more bodhisattva day, "Who are we to judge who you pick, Mali, but they have to be at your level, they have to understand who you are." When Yusuf says, in response to a photo of Deeta paying bills under the fake chandelier the previous owners, Holocaust survivors, put in, "high rollers, huh," and I tell him my father didn't grow up famous like his or protected like him, he rolls onto that splintered back. "Mali, you know what it's like to come from a place like that? Forget about me. You've got to get out of here and do something with yourself for him."

The 1:30 p.m. bus is nowhere to be seen and Yusuf's figure has almost smoked out into the wavy heat, going to or from the casinos I'll never know. But from his turn away, after each of us have side-eyed the other, I hear what we've been trying to say: how all blues, whether his or mine or some long-gone woman's, are not at all the same.

One Tiny Thing

ROSES

Ramu's grace saved my ass that summer. I was standing in a Davis lavender patch when Ramu pulled his Corolla up to the corner: "Nepali? Name? Job?" Two months after my voice coaching degree and still nothing: "Assamese, Nirmali, wanted." When Tashi stuck her peach face out the window, I clasped her good hand and added, "Sure, why not." How could I know I'd be biking for months between a restaurant and a mansion, their family and the Subrahmanians? All I knew was you couldn't go home again.

Every evening, Ramu overgrinned at Gerald that I "outworked the guys": the Nepali best-bud chefs who had been lawyers in Kathmandu, the Laotian bodybuilder who pointed out his Hanuman necklace as he dreamily washed each plate, the Oaxacan servers who smiled *muy bonita* for every question but who seemed skittish in their own skin. I stayed pissed—pouring red wine for white, letting my tie dip into curries I set before customers—and couldn't understand how Gerald sat meditatively morning and evening by the bamboo vats, eating bowls of strawberry ice cream.

"Mali, how many plates you broke today? I may have to fine you."

"Good luck finding another Indian to work here. Indians can tell when you don't like their food, you know."

He licked his spoon carefully. "What do you mean? Do you know how many people want your job?"

Back in her kitchen, Ma had refused to let me cook—*you don't need to be like me*—but in Delhi Delight, I rinse blades, turn up the stove fire, listen with shut eyes to Tashi gliding about the kitchen. She's got a shuffle steadier than mine, and I imagine her in nurse days, scouring germs from sick rooms, sliding along halls unseen, a face not quite Indian enough. Like and unlike Ma, who swished through our house a hell-bent hawk for twenty years, collecting lucky pennies off the street. Every afternoon, Ma made me and Henna puddle our school clothes at the door, before we ate pithas and apples at the kitchen table, jubilantly comparing our crystalline slices in the streaming light.

When I tell Tashi I barely speak to Ma and Henna, that Mrs. Subrahmanian treats me like the village idiot, Tashi smiles as if, really, I'm a stand-up comedian. "Not loving like you, huh?" She unclenches my fists, slips the bone and fork from them onto my plate, and lines our seven plates along her arms. She walks, amid the bustle of men in aprons, backward to the kitchen sink, her left foot dragging a route through the linoleum suds. *She can't ever escape*, I think. *All her friends, all her enemies would find her.*

I scrub vats beside her, the tap spray soothing my aching wrists, while the men stack cup and napkin pyramids and Gerald thumblicks tips behind the register.

"Aren't you going to the casino with the guys?" I say.

"Listen, young lady." He presses a finger to my forehead. "Gambling is for poor and rich men. Do I look like poor and rich men to you?"

I think of Kosal who, in the first days, brought me bowls of ramen he'd saved from Sushi Express stints, designer-name jackets he'd bartered for weed and whatnot, then tucked about my chin.

Kosal of the fantasy eyes and promises who, in the last days, stalked me on grocery errands, on café dates, before disappearing on dirt bike trails, on all-boy-benders for weeks.

"Lots of people spend money they don't have," I say and Gerald turns his vested back on me.

After the restaurant closes, I help Tashi shake out a pink cotton sheet, dotted with elephants, on her living room carpet, and when she insists on carrying the plates of beef momos, the ginger tea alone, I wait between the lumpy sofas, before a TV with the kind of old-school dial Ma had kept working with a folded paper wedge. Each upper wall is rimmed with a gold-tasseled tapestry of round-bellied gods and an altar of dried roses and singing bowls sits crammed between the TV and a photo column of the Dalai Lama, glasses on, glasses off, grin forever on. That's the only fancy, not like the Subrahmanians' mansion in the gated part of town, where I'd been given a tour of their wood slat contraption with its front plot of long-stemmed, plump reds. "Our roses," the little girl had said as I'd unlocked my bike from a pipe, "raise the property value."

"The woman is a crappy mom," I say as Tashi rotates her steaming teacup. "She shows up at twelve on the dot, sits at the kitchen table eating her sandwich, and the baby goes crawling to her from the living room."

Tashi presses her claw to her chest.

"Then she tells me to go play with her and the toys. A baby doesn't want toys! She wants her mommy!"

"What does on the dot mean?"

"Oh, it means exactly on time. You're never a minute early or late."

Tashi forks a momo in half, and its blood rushes out: cilantro, pepper, meat tendrils. "Have to strike while it's hot, Tara!"

Which is Ramu's line, before he jets for the casino on Wednesdays, though that's not why I tense forward. "Who?"

Tashi lifts her claw to her lips, as if they're burning. "Mali," she says, clinking her tea cup with mine. "Happy New Year."

M is For

Kosal would call one minute after noon, himself on lunch break at Golden Bear Bikes, and name a hundred reasons to get on social media. "It's hard for all of us right now," he'd say. "At least you know how to hustle, at least you got your degrees." "But where's that getting any of us," I'd say, chewing the PBJ and slurping the Sprite I'd bagged. "And you know these liberals can be racist as fuck." Kosal would pause then, neither of us bringing up my voice peers who won't acknowledge him at parties or his hipster friends who sing about revolution but talk over me at concerts, before saying, "Listen, I got to run, there's a customer."

A month later, Kosal gone again, I will still be feather-dusting chairs in the Subrahmanian mansion, still be lifting Nena up by her armpits, still be caught breathless on rare evenings I call and Ma snorts, "A maid is what you are." *Not for long,* I want to say, along with a number for every window ad, every Craigslist link to which I'd sent my resume and got crickets back. "I'm trying," I say instead, not disclosing details like the time the light-skinned Latina in the one ethnic kitsch store saw my brown face, widened her eyes, and swiped the applications off the counter: "Sorry, we're all out." "You never did that stuff at home," Ma says, meaning she had, from the day she landed as a no-English bride to the day she shouldered our suitcases into college dorms, before finally slapping a blue-apron magnet on our humming fridge: *M is for mom, not maid.*

At every afternoon's end, I arrange the magnets and Post-its on Mrs. Subrahmanian's fridge with care—so that she cannot say I stole this or that thing as she has said of teabags she initially offered—a fridge as steely as her unblinking stare from evening one. She'd corralled her clan, one of Davis's IT Indians, to the back table by the restaurant bathroom, away from the snotty undergrads— *Look! All hands! Like a savage!*—and the trashed men with cut-eye girlfriends, both of whom studied my chest. An hour into their plates of salmon and biryani, Mrs. Subrahmanian hailed me over to examine the water, which she held up, a glowing yellow under the hanging lamp. "Do you see what I see?" Her stern moon face reminded me of my mother's, except she sounded hopeful, like I might have a good explanation.

"Do you see what I see?" the curly-haired girl beside her sang, flashing me a gap-toothed grin. Mrs. Subrahmanian watched the baby, who'd stopped thumping her high chair to stare at me. "She likes you."

Her husband sipped the yellow water. "You look patient. We're looking for a nanny."

"I have zero experience."

"Experience no bar," she said.

"Unless," Gerald said, carrying over glasses of clear water, "it's my bar."

Which is how I end up dangling Nena at arm's length every 8:00 a.m., crinkling my nose at her durian-stink diapers, before glass doors the expanse of their kitchen wall. What if I'd spoken up that evening: *I hate babies, never had 'em, never was one?* Maybe I wouldn't be starting my day running down tasks Mrs. Subrahmanian has posted on the fridge, organizing a living room quadruple the size of mine when I was Megan's age. Two white leather sofas; a wall-sized TV and remote control stereo system; another wall of stuffed zebras, Tahitian Barbies, and enough Legos to build a mini-Cadillac, toys Nena picks through before hurling them, with banshee whoops, into the middle of the room. Whereas we'd had a yellow-and-purple rug-like thing atop whatever shaggy carpet in whichever mixed-income neighborhood in the central Bronx, the Subrahmanians have carpeted all four bedrooms in ivory white, which, by lunch, I'm vacuuming against the AC so as to fly under the local noise ordinance. And whereas Deeta had placed two king-sized mattresses by each other, Henna punching me in her sleep as I shivered for the covers, and Ma had stocked the other bedroom with English novels and Assamese buranjis, the Subrahmanians have in their guest bedroom one bookshelf thinly stocked with computer programming manuals, Jhumpa Lahiri stories, and a Hawaii travel guide. I leave the adjacent spare room for afternoon's end when, as I once did, Megan spills a hundred crayons on a mahogany table, except hers come from a wooden box with a silver clasp and she draws pages and pages of her, Nena, and her father. Mrs. Subrahmanian is nowhere to be found in Megan's paper imagination, just as she's absent on the payday I wait in the kitchen, pouring cups of hot water for her forlorn trio.

A computer engineer like his wife, Mr. Subrahmanian is one of those laidback, dusky nerds who's chosen a light-skinned socialite that's dreamt of America as much as a husband. He stands formally behind the chair as I set a plate of powdery tea cookies. "Do you like it here? What did you study?"

"Teaching jobs for voice and speech are hard to come by."

"My wife is married to her work. Sit."

Megan clambers onto my lap and stuffs a cookie into her mouth, and Mr. Subrahmanian eases into the opposite chair. "You must miss home."

"The program gave me a full ride. So I came."

"There were a lot of Assamese in Bangalore. They work hard."

"Contrary to popular opinion," I say but he doesn't laugh.

"They aren't always treated well." He raises Nena from her high chair, where she has been staring at me again, and says, "Don't stay long. You should find suitable work, suitable home." He doesn't say suitable husband like Ramu, who jokes that I need a mountain man but will end up with a clueless American, asking instead, "does anyone visit?"

Because the names before Kosal's—overconfident white boys with geisha fever and liberal arts degrees, chip-shouldered black boys with lightskin fever and hardknock knowledges—can't be pronounced here, I shrug. "I go when I can."

Mr. Subrahmanian peers into his tea, his girls draping themselves over his shoulders with a possessiveness I'll never know again, and says, "What are your family's names?"

Gulapi, Hollong, Henna. I haven't recited these names since leaving New York, but just as I'm about to say *Rose, Tree, Crushed Leaf,* Mrs. Subrahmanian strolls in and, without glancing at me, touches Mr. Subrahmanian's dark pate. "I've been waiting extra," I say and, when she finally blinks, I murmur, "Mali is short for Nirmali, an offering to appease the gods."

Careless

As I biked between my apartment in the old-pipes part of town and the Subrahmanians' chateau in the gated part, I'd pass cop cars circling campus. Kids I'd once taught held signs up that read *stop privatization, no more tuition hikes, take back our UC,* along the oblong quad that had once seemed forever coniferous and sedate. I pumped past chanting crowds on one side of the green, somber trapezoid buildings on the other, glad I'd gotten out the year before but not sure we hadn't all been caught in a dream gone wrong.

This afternoon, instead of sampling tater tots I've plated, Megan climbs onto the marble sink counter and hollers about rifles and yellow men from "Born in the U.S.A."

"Megan, please," I say as she rocks side-to-side like a tow boat. "Megan, there are knives to your left *and* to your right. If you slip, you could fall into the sink, onto a knife, or on the floor."

Megan yanks down her jeans, swing it around her head like a lasso, then hops from one foot to another as she sings a few bars of welcome from "Hotel California." Nena crawls before the sink, and sits clapping and cooing.

I catch Megan's flailing arms and pull her down, then, squatting, arrange Nena on one hip and yank floor-magnet Megan, singing even louder of prisoners in "Hotel California." Through the dining room, down the long hall, up the stairs, into the bath—Megan shadow-boxing my words as we race.

"Why're you acting so crazy?"

"Say something that makes sense!"

"This is no time for games—grow up!"

As the tub fills with foaming water, Megan faces the wall, bends over, and slaps her bum. "Big butt darkie!" She flaps her elbows like chicken wings.

"Megan." I snap off the water and pull her by the elbow to face me. "Is someone saying these things to you?"

Megan has a grin so tightly stretched over her face, it's almost a prize sticker someone's given her. She scrunches her eyes and takes a soldier stance, saluting some invisible flag, and sings *bigbuttdarkie, bigbuttdarkie, bigbuttdarkie . . .*

I wrap her in the shell towel, so that the sound is muffled, but she snatches at my boobs.

"Listen to me, devil-child. You're beautiful but you're bad."

She doesn't respond, not like my child self, who'd run weeping into closets if I suspected Deeta had taken Henna out without me. One sister the display color of cream, the other the shameful color of earth; one more reason I conjecture Ma prefers Henna who looks like her to me who, she once told Deeta, was *her father's daughter.* I wipe Megan's unblemished skin and think of the crescent scar marking my left hip crease, where Ma and Henna had thrown that plate at me, a calendar they can't erase since they can no longer touch me.

The other devil-child flings her rubber duck at my back and Megan throws her arms about my neck, laughing. "You hear that, baby? D-e-v . . ."

Though I'm the one who confesses our names, months later on a pine-rimmed lawn, carved pumpkins dotted about like crushed heads. Megan, Nena, and I slump on a wooden bench under a willow, before Megan's sprawling stone elementary school, *Institute for The Gifted.* Mrs. Subrahmanian always pronounced it syllabically, her voice pitching up rather than trailing off. *Institute for The Gild-*

ed, I'd told Ma the first night back, and she'd snorted. "Well, they can afford it. But no one can buy actual brains or manners."

Watching the other kids whisked away, for an hour by drivers and nannies, I wasn't so sure. They'd flown across the grass in spotless sneakers and Burberry pea coats, into BMWs and Mercedes the lustrous hues of blood and pearls. I'd hoisted up Nena and hand-dragged Megan to the jungle gym behind the school, and thought, as I plopped Nena on the wood chips, *a proper childhood means getting dirty. It means*, I thought as I lifted Megan onto the monkey bars, *learning to play alone.*

A svelte Davis type strolls up with her blonde Cabbage Patch baby as I stand one leg in each sand box, between Nena the high horn and Megan the trapeze artist. "Are they yours?"

Nena is digging a hole in the wood chips, perhaps also hoping to cross to a better side of the planet. "I'm the nanny," I say and Megan presses her hands in namaste to her heart. "Nearly live-in . . ." Megan lets go one leg and swings her other limbs like a godforsaken spider. "She's babysitter number four!"

The woman laughs. "Is that who you are!"

I clear my throat for my elevator pitch on voice coaching, but Megan resumes humming—about impossible escape from "Hotel California"—and Ms. Fancy Detective strain-smiles and strollers her baby, who's reaching fists out to Megan, away from the sandboxes to the curb, where a gaggle of moms in glossy spandex compare sneaker soles.

An hour later, curb and lot swept of Davis housewives and piled with dried leaves, Mrs. Subrahmanian pulls up—I step out relieved from behind the willow, Nena asleep on the picnic table to its left, Megan sprawled in a Ralph Lauren romper on the muddy grass—and squints exponentially smaller as she saunters, then strides over. She barely responds to my wave, just curls her upper lip and slaps chips off both girls' frocks. When her hands touch dog poop, I can't help giggling at the tremors that seize her suited frame.

"How could you let them get so dirty? Do you know what these Americans say about Indian people?"

"We waited two hours," I say.

She starts, then turns toward the school doors, every overhead letter of its title promise glistening in late sun. "We waited two hours and they wouldn't eat what I brought and Megan has no friends." She drags Megan away from me—*that Thai girl* she calls me publicly, *that crazy girl* she probably calls me privately—I stomp after her holding Nena who, for once, stays asleep.

As I rev up the car, I say, "*Of course* I know what Americans say. I grew up here, remember?"

Mrs. Subrahmanian chooses not to reply, just dials an IT friend on the phone, and streams forth in Telegu with English flags of "Nanny, uncontrollable, overwhelmed." I careen the car down the road—swerving right here—"Girls!"—swerving left there—"Nirmali!"—with a roaring pedal that makes us seem trapped inside an engine.

Nena wakes up and screams.

I swerve left again, across an oncoming van that just misses our tail—Mrs. Subrahmanian drops the phone and grabs the wheel, my right arm. "Are you trying to kill us all?"

Just you, I want to say but she bends under the dashboard, as if hiding from snipers, and exclaims into the phone, "What did I tell you!"

"Okay, breathe," she mutters. "Calm, calm."

When I pull into the Subrahmanians' driveway, right against those sumptuous roses, she slams the car door and marches with the girls into the stately wood-arched door of that wood-slatted house. For several minutes, we're at crosswinds, my lugging duffel bags and baby seaters onto the porch while she pretends to inspect both bumpers, the taillights, the driver's seat until standing cross-armed on the steps. I'm back in my parents' car, some dark Honda model with door scratches, in yet another run-in. Sometimes, it would be a car Deeta had tail-sped into, sometimes a head-on Ma had left-turned across. Mostly, it was their front seat arguing that spilled out at a gas station or roadside curb: "Stupid! Irresponsible! Don't tell me what to do!" Henna and I cowered in the back seat, me holding her on rides she sobbed, neither of us sure the most common refrain wasn't also meant for us: "How could you be so careless?" We'd look around at an unsigned highway, a dandelioned field, unsure if we wanted the police to familiarize this country too.

Today, however, it is Mrs. Subrahmanian who walks over as I unlock my bike from her Davis gas pipe.

"I wrote a little extra for all the waiting," she says, handing me the week's check with a doubled amount. "I hope that is fair."

"Thank you," I whisper.

"You know," she says evenly as I straddle the bike seat, "no one can love the way a mother loves." I turn away from this lie I never learned, staring straight at the roses, hoping she will tell me to never, ever come near her babies. "I'll see you tomorrow morning?" she says.

I drag the bike back step by step and say, "Yes, of course, I'll be there."

Later that night, Ma says, "you still can't say no, can you?"

"And who," I say, "did I learn that from?"

Though Ma is the one who hangs up, I tingle on my floor mattress as if it were as wooden as the floor, as if I were the one who had shut her out first, as if any old house could be called shelter could be called home.

Everything is Funny

Wednesday dinner shifts, the guys stream back to the bistro, giddy with beer and momentary wins. Their bragging fills the brown dining area like a secret music—Ramu detailing how he wrangled five hundred dollars at the tables, the Laotian singing how he played the slot machines for two hundred dollars—all as they slap out fresh tablecloths, set glasses facedown with a swift delicacy. I trail them, framing each plate with silverware, and wonder how much they made once upon another life. Ramu the lawyer in Kathmandu, the Laotian a construction manager in Vientiane, Gerald a business-man even in Bangkok.

This is the one day of the week Gerald never scolds the guys. He just swims in his pink shirt between the dining area, the nar-row kitchen, the well-lit bar, and hums with thumbs in his trouser pockets.

"You still not going with them?" I say.

He turns from the wine bottles he's re-lining on the bar and frowns. "The vegan customers have said you told them to try next door or next year. Is this true?"

I laugh. "My question first."

He sighs over-long, as if I'm a spiritual trial, and muscles open a corked Riesling. "Beggars can't be gamblers." He peers over the red wineglass. "But maybe if you went and won, you could afford a new shirt and some food."

Ramu waves me over to his vat of eggplant curry and whispers as he stirs. "Don't mind Gerald. That's just his talk. You know how long I lived in this country for? Ten years without a proper coat or car." He scrapes the bubbly stew into a rectangular plastic contain-er. "It was hard, Mali. So many women want to be with me. I'm good-looking, right?" He drops the spoon to pat his thinning waves. "So many beautiful, beautiful women, you don't know. But," he claps his chest. "I remember my wife. So see? I can give up women, I can give up smoking. But," he fishes out a few peppery-scented cubes and ladles them into a Styrofoam cup he passes to me. "I can't give up chasing the luck."

That evening, at Ramu's place for the anniversary party, I want to ask Tashi if she and Ramu had left Kathmandu because of the Mao-ists or the money. But the one-bedroom apartment is so jammed with cousins and uncles and kids—drinking on the couches, running down the hall, hand-holding forth stories—that I plop down on the living room sheet. I'm never going to leave. Ramu, full face-flushed, raises his beer can. "Right on Indian Standard Time. One hour late!"

Tashi glides out the kitchen in a rose silk kurta, looking like she's known these people, who look nothing like her, since birth. "Mali," she says, piling a paper plate of pea pullao, saag paneer, and mutton chunks before I can say *no*, "Come with me."

Seven kids crowd Tashi's computer in the bedroom, looking for fun just as we used to apart from adults, but they click on a martial arts video game with a Lara Croft figure that hadn't existed then. Ma wouldn't have let us play anyway, and when Tashi pulls one boy up by his ear from her chair, the other kids shuffle out like a spell, making as little protest as I had in what Henna calls my better days. "It's for a nursing program here," Tashi says of the file she opens, her claw gripping the mouse so tightly the skin turns as purple as Ramu's face. "They won't accept the India degree."

I want to ask if I can do this another day but, perusing the first lines, I sigh: *When I was born in Darjeeling, where my parents go because of Chinese, my family has too many girls. I came early and small, so my mother did not think I will live. She leaves me on fireplace in empty room.*

"No problem," I say and drift the mouse arrow over her script: *I was there in cold too many days, so my left side does not develop like right. But Miss Kamala, an older neighbor who never marries, saved my life. She fed me with cow's milk. She convince my parents I am worth raising. She become like my own sister.*

Tashi sits calmly on the bed, spreading all around her the blood-red wedding invitations for Ramu's nephew, paper fold-outs hiding Ganesh, his belly and trunk curved with pleasure.

My parents kept me at home because I work hard, and there was no money for a girl who cannot marry. But I read to myself at night or with Miss Kamala, after taking care of house, in kitchen with candles.

When my parents put me in school, everyone made fun, saying I am old, lame, and girl. But I say back, it is exactly because of this I will finish.

I click-clack away at her grammar, inserting polite notes about *place details here* and *describe schooling there,* though the truth I can't type sensibly is *talk about what drove your folks from Tibet, talk about what brought you here.*

When I am in nursing school, I must work twice as hard as men, and even girls move faster than me. They have connections in city. But I won't quit and go back home after to start nutrition classes. I start reading program so other girls can stay in school. When I go back to city, I take shifts no one wants, and this is how I last longer, how I have more skills. This is why I am strong candidate for your program.

I swivel in the chair and say, "What's the difference between arranged marriage and love marriage? You guys obviously aren't arranged."

"That is like asking what is love," Tashi says, and I don't tell her what Ma used to say. How she'd met Deeta once the month before their wedding: "Ata let me choose." I don't tell Tashi about the mornings Ma dazed through soap operas and uninvited guest-cooking or evenings she meditated, an arm over her eyes, beside windows that faced yards of Dobermans and squash blossoms and someone else's dark kids. I definitely don't tell Tashi I don't want what she's got, an apartment where things come and go, one day the armory, the next day the clock, or a man so charming night stars drop into my eyes and I can't navigate that rare country, a love marriage.

"Actually, it's like asking for love recipes," I say.

Tashi presses herself up and drags over a phone book she casts beside the invites. "Practice for our interviews. America-born legal assistants must also speak perfectly." So I slip beside the love mounds and fold umpteen invites until Tashi points to an ad for litigation. "Am I saying this right?" She reads the boisterous offer for legal counsel for anyone who's been framed in a gentle tone, stuttering over the word *fraudulent*. When I laugh, she looks up. "You would never make a good lawyer. You think everything is funny."

We fold a whole other mound of invites when Tashi says, "Ramu used to be part of a group of boys who would follow me from the hospital where I did my nursing work. They used to call me the lame *chinku* and copy the way I walked, the whole way back. For an hour."

My palms freeze above a new mound.

"A whole hour," Tashi says, flattening the mound with her claw. "Every evening. I thought, they will get tired, they will get bored, they will not rape me because they hate me."

I don't want to hear the rest.

"But I learn you can do both. One evening when the other girls weren't there, when only two of the guys were there, I learn you can do both."

I draw my sweaty palms onto my lap.

"When Ramu heard, he visited me at the hospital. I could see, unlike the others, something touched him. I'm not sure what it was but he started coming every day. We weren't friends then, just trying to walk past this." Tashi pulls her own hands onto her lap and stares at them.

"Tashi."

She shakes her head. "Then one day, walking that same road from the hospital, with Ramu next to me, not behind me, I knew." She presses herself up and smiles at me inexplicably, her peach face flush again. "See? No recipe."

I walk to the threshold between the bedroom, the kitchen, and the living room, where the guests are strumming old Bollywood songs on a guitar—I'm rushed back to one of those New Jersey fêtes where some uncle pulled out a harmonium and sang of the hungry river, of disappeared loves, of Assamese freedom—and I wonder which parts of Tashi's essay, Ma's biography, or my own memories are true? "Listen long enough to the silences," the voice teachers used to say, "and the beast will show its face." Already half the folks sway as they hold each other, the other half clap in beat. I don't hear Tashi's bright contralto, her peculiar accent among them, but she's easy to spot, her unabashed smile up at Ramu, whose own eyes are closed as if traveling somewhere more mountainous and green. The way her claw cups and claims his right shoulder, the way her good hand traces each of his palms, his wrists, inside and out, circle after circle, she might as well be the loudest one in the room.

SPEED

"Lipoma," the X-ray technician had said matter of factly, as I lay quivering in the sonic tunnel. "Seven centimeters and growing." He pressed a finger to the eggish mass behind my right knee and tapped about, as if looking for a chick within that might respond. Back in the bunker I rent, in a purple hippie house with doors that never close, I google "tumor." The images, laid out like some grotesque checkerboard, are pink-red-white, though few veined gems are as large as mine. Maybe this is why strangers would pause me on the street, "Do you know you have a lump? You should get it checked." "There are so many ways to go," I'd say, "speed is just a detail." When I call the Bronx, Deeta says, "A lipoma is not a tumor, that is what we had." I want to scream, "Do you know which house I live in, what has happened in yours?" But I say, "I can barely bend my knee, what if surgery hobbles me?" To which Ma says, "You have to learn to live with this." Which means I can never ask "How do I cut this out for good" from a woman who's expelled me more than once from what others call family. I will never hear her say, as she would to Henna, "Come home, we will find a way to heal this."

I pick up more work with Ramu instead, a weekend after I learn the name for what I've got, this time for his nephew's reception, a marriage Tashi refuses to label. Ramu's got his usual dapper on— white shirt, ironed slacks—weaving quickly between the waiters, tired-seeming Mexican Indians, in the long and churning rectangle of the Veteran's Hall. Still Ramu, who must have come hours before to set up the folding tables, to prep veggies and knives in the kitchen, stops now and then to tease a child in a puffy dress, to confer with one of the waiters, to reheat the samosas or naan. He stands straight, shielding his eyes for Tashi, who watches from a corner table—as if this is the life he's wanted all along.

Tashi and I sit by the entrance, which is closer for her to the restrooms and better for introducing me to folks who stream in and speak to us in Nepali. Tashi, eyes crinkled in glee, has to tell them I don't understand. A drunk old uncle whispers hotly in my ear, "I pretend to be things too." I flinch, half-expecting The Ass Slap but the bhangra starts playing, he jabs his pointer finger in the air, and limps over to the small circle of dancers forming by our table. Tashi smiles as he swing-taps his left metal calf, jiggles out his skinny arms and un-ringed hands, and says, "He reminds me so much of my father."

"The crazy moves?"

"My dad lost his leg crossing from Tibet to India. His feet turned totally black from the snow. They had no time, you know, when the Chinese came." She strokes her own left leg. "He never complained, not even when his hip ached. The only thing he said was, even if they took both feet, I would walk back if they let me."

I blush, remembering how I'd whined to Kosal that I couldn't bend my knee, how I'd never again dance carefree. Kosal who had pinched the lump behind my knee, then both my cheeks, had said, *I'll love you no matter what, Nirmali*, words I haven't learned to trust or receive. Instead I draw Tashi's good hand into mine. "I got the job."

Her eyes flutter wide—the hall chandeliers reflected like bright mandalas—and she says wistfully, "good things will happen for you, huh?"

Because I hear the tart note of Ma and Biju when I relay any hopeful thing, I take her other hand. "I got a tumor diagnosis too. It's not cancer but I don't know how I'll move after surgery."

Unexpectedly, Tashi's eyes fill up, mandalas receding behind rapid blinking, and she says, "Why do the good suffer and the rich get everything?"

I wish I knew the answer or how to thank her for slipping good next to my name, so I say, "Let's dance."

She shakes her head but I pull her up anyways, over to Uncle, who grasps her arms tightly as he jiggles that metal leg, I stomp my growing one, and Tashi shuts her eyes and sways.

Later, as the dinner crowd starts thinning, Ramu and I collect stray forks from the tables, rinse emptied trays in the sink. We're basking in the thrumming quiet, foiling up leftover rice and chicken, when he says, "You know we had a daughter?"

I stop packing the cauliflower pakoras and turn, but Ramu's already peering into the fridge, his narrow back bent over the lowest shelf, unreadable. "Once upon a time," he laughs lightly. "Isn't that how fairy tales begin?"

"Ramu." I step towards him, the dishes in each of my hands dripping onto the floor.

He turns, his goodtime grin taut over his face, and swipes the plate from my left hand. "You know India. Rickshaw: upside-down"—and drops the plate—SMASH!—smithereens flying to irretrievable ends of the kitchen. "Strangers won't help. Doctors won't help. Even God won't help." He crouches now to pick up the largest shards around our feet, then thuds them into the trash can by the sink.

"What was her name?"

He squeezes drip from a sponge and slowly wipes spirals into the sink.

"Is that what happened to Tashi's leg?"

He bends again—something he never does, he's told me, because the work will kill your feet and your back—looking so deeply down the drain, his neck bones jut up like a tiny head.

"Fifteen years," he says. "My wife still wakes up and says she sees our daughter crushed under her."

We foil-wrap the rest of the leftovers—lumpy fritters, eggplant hash, marrow-spilling bones—in silence that throbs, and under the fluorescent lights everything takes on the rumpled skin, the scrambled insides of a dead child. I do not know how Ramu handles these things nightly.

I imagine asking Ramu for a news brief, but for every tray I slip into the fridge, it's my own interrogation I draft.

Where? I will sit up in bed, fortressed under covers, and Google photos of camps. Who got moved to some strange Where—Treblinka, Kinshasa, Dharamsala—the eye will shatter over dots of folks spreading across train, savannah, hill.

What? I will strain facial muscles like those men's in World War I hospital wards. Men staring tautly at the camera, their chopped limbs bandaged in gauze, the brightest detail of those black-and-white squares.

Who? Refugees, exiles, runaways, I will explain. They often look as if they're teetering between wanting to kill you or themselves, but don't have the willpower for either mercy.

When? How will I describe the look on my mother's face, a heart I have not seen in seven hundred thirty days? In what language will I say *I can't stomach your food, I hate coming home, this time I'm running away for good*?

Why? I will answer promptly: they will say you don't belong, because here-you-go-you-are-marked, because this land is (suddenly) ours, because we have evolved and therefore we must live, we must stay, we must feast on whatever you leave behind.

How? I will enumerate: gelatinous orbs and sore pink stubs. Rifles, batons, rods, any recyclable metal thing. Spoonfuls of nerve-shot artery, gut, clit. Dangling gold chains and family amulets. Packets of singed hair, ashes, bones.

Clutching a sponge that's dripping from crud I've cleared off counter tops, I say, "Some people lose daughters, some mothers, some sisters."

"Your only problem is too many rules," Ramu says. "You need someone quick-quick, a free spirit like me!"

So I can be as stable as Tashi, I want to ask, but Ramu is already heading where she sits, on a lone fold-out chair, before the deejay who coils up the electrical cords. She never looks at us, though our voices must carry, just kneads her hands as if the show were in fact beginning.

ONE TINY THING

Henna and I no longer call for birthdays, hers the midnight before October, but I imagine her cradling her own firstborn in the Bronx bedroom where we'd whispered our dreams. Whereas I'm lugging and rocking Nena around the Subrahmanian cage, up, down, room to room, except today Nena whimpers all morning as if for us both. So that by two, Nena crying in fitful spurts, shivering in a sweat I can't ease with milk or moist washcloths, I dial the mother I trust most.

Strange sweetness to open the door: Tashi, hair slicked into a bun, cracking her knuckles as if about to break wood. Though she's sporting new blue slacks, a florid blouse Ramu must've bought, she deftly slips off her flats, rolls up her cuffs, and trails me to the kitchen sink. "Take me to your leader."

Tashi laughs at Nena burping and splashing like a content frog in the salad bowl. "This is what you're serving, huh?"

I imagine Mrs. Subrahmanian's icy manners disintegrating if I were to place tongs beside Nena during, say, her lunch hour ritual. "Don't tempt me."

"Where's the medicine cabinet?" Tashi says, wrapping Nena in green dishrags as she whimpers and fist-shivers again. I lead Tashi through the candelabraed dining room, across and up the master bedroom with its red silk curtains, its mahogany bureau of wedding china, silver-framed portraits, and snow globes from London, Sydney, Dubai, all sorts of cities we've never been.

"Wow," Tashi runs one finger along the deep rose varnish, never looking up at the mirror. She examines her pointer—no dust—I'd made sure of that.

I take Nena, who's nodding for the first time all day, and lay her gently on the bed.

Like a slow top, Tashi is turning, surveying—the wide, tasseled bed, the walk-in closet of shoes and ties, the opened boxes of computer gadgets that will get unabashedly lugged back—"they're well-off, huh?"

"They're computer engineers," I say. "The husband drives a motorcycle all over this town." I roll my eyes at a wannabe hero in Aviators vrooming past pastures of cows and sheep.

Tashi steps towards one of the four cabinets that lines the door wall and opens the leftmost door. Then the next door. Then each drawer. Of every single cabinet. She moves deliberately, like someone in a trance, while I sit on the bed, patting Nena's rising-falling belly. For several minutes, there is no other sound but the baby's phlegmy breath and the *swish-thump* of doors and drawers opening and closing, so that if I'd closed my eyes, I might've been out by the riled-up sea by our riled-up house.

Dropping on her good knee, Tashi guesses at the medicine drawer, opening the lower left latch of the last bureau. The bottles are all mixed up with a stash of lingerie and, as Tashi lifts it up gingerly, a set of handcuffs.

"What is this doing here?" she says.

Mrs. Subrahmanian, you sneaky lady, I grin, and wonder who does what to whom. I kneel beside Tashi and pull out a frilly purple camisole. "Try it on."

Tashi hesitates and fingers the frill.

"No one's looking," I say. "Come on. When else are you gonna wear this?"

Tashi stretches out her left leg and rubs it, as if the answer is pulsing there. She gleans off her tee in a swift tug, arches back to peel off one jean leg, then another. Her form, this close-up, is unsurprisingly peach-soft and startlingly opalesque. She pushes herself up, grunting, and as she stands, crooked to the right as always to ease her left weight, in just her wide cotton bra and panties, her smooth back lines, her slender, scarred legs read like the statue of a Tibetan deity no one's yet dug up. *Poor Megan*, I think as Tashi unwraps her bra, *she's gonna miss some breasts.*

Tashi's breasts are longer than I would've guessed from her quaint blouses, almost gold gourds, and for a moment, Nena's breath drops to a hum. *Ah, here's one thing that keeps Ramu close.* Tashi slips on the purple camisole, the transparent cups barely covering her silver dollar nipples, and she murmurs, "Even after babies, she's this size?"

I know this game—I've played it aplenty with rich girls—measuring my wealth against theirs.

"If my chest looked like yours," I say, "she'd probably ask me to breastfeed Nena too." I hand Tashi a larger, lacy black bra. The price tag still dangles from the back—seventy-five dollars—but Tashi wraps it easily around herself, the cups fitting as if they were made for her. She shifts side to side, a smile creeping over her face, her hand resting on the upper slope of her tummy, and when I say, "too bad Ramu isn't here," she laughs. Just as slowly, she unsnaps the bra, slides each strap down her arm, and shakes her head as the bra drops to her plain panty.

"What am I doing?"

"Take it!"

"Oh, no, no, no." Tashi tugs off the bra, as if my words were dark magic, and fumbles on her tee.

"Tashi, she has a hundred! In a couple months, even the smaller ones won't fit her."

Tashi turns her back to the mirror and frowns at me. "Nirmali, you think we need more bad karma?"

I flush at *we* and hand Tashi the blue medicine bag, lumpy with bottles of pills and lotions. Tashi plucks out the Tylenol, crushes it between her thumb and pinky, and sprinkles half into the milk bottle she's left on the bureau. Nena squirms when Tashi lifts her up but settles glossy-eyed into her thick-armed hold, her bottle-soothing song. As if singing to herself, in Tibetan or Nepali I can't tell, Tashi wanders out with the baby into the hall. Her lullaby drifts in from various rooms as I slump on the bed, staring at ajar drawers, the scattered bras, the necklaces draped over knobs that I'll have to tidy up again.

I slide down to the carpet and pluck up the discarded black bra, cradling it in both hands like an unexpected jewel; would Mrs. Subrahmanian really notice if this were gone? I roll the bra up into a ball so soft yet dense, it could be my lump. *Couldn't Tashi have this one tiny thing, for all the things taken from her in other days?* I think as I stuff the ball into my back pocket.

Tashi shuffles back, just as I slap the first drawer shut, and sets a dozing Nena on the bed. She hugs herself, chest sloped in, as if the house and baby-holding have knocked the heat from her. "You should quit. The signs are everywhere."

"I keep trying but she won't agree, no matter what I do."

"What kind of parent," Tashi says, dropping her arms, trembling up on her tippie-toes to stretch her good leg, then her left leg slowly, squinting through the window onto that lush rose patch, "leaves her most valuable possession with someone who can't take care of it?"

FALLEN

When I'd knocked on her door that afternoon, Megan stumbled out of bed, eyes swollen like a fly's, whisper spitting my elbow.

"Can you please read me a story?" It's the Friday before Diwali, the Hindu holiday when Good triumphs over Evil, but I'm stuck in the upstairs bedroom while Mrs. Subrahmanian paces about, dumping each room's linen in a hallway mound. Sucks to read *The Little Prince* a hundred times, repeating mantras that seem lost not only on my boss but my life.

It is the time wasted for your rose that makes your rose so important.

Megan nods off on the hundredth recitation and the walls buzz with the back-and-forth of Mrs. Subrahmanian's vacuum.

Walking in a straight line, one cannot get very far.

I remember blocks I circled as a child, counting geraniums resiliently red on apartment stairwells, marigolds abloom in the front plot Deeta had taught us to hoe, flowers nowhere to be found in this valley heat.

You become responsible forever, and as I flip the page on this omen that ends *for what you have tamed,* Megan shoves up to drink her ginger ale and I feel the surge. Acidic, sulfurous, shooting up my windpipe, burning from my nostrils through my head. I rush to Megan's bathroom and, kneeling over the toilet, *hack!* A green snake dribbles out my mouth. *Aargh!* a tide of morning bagel-egg-apple pours out.

"Mali?" Megan stands at the doorway, eyes blinking rapidly. "Are you sick too?"

I sit to the side of the toilet and rest my head between my knees. "I'm just tired, Megan. Go back to bed."

Megan runs downstairs, cup still in hand, and says, "Daddy! Mali's fallen on the floor!"

The surges are coming faster now, as if a squall were releasing inside, and I have to hang directly over the toilet bowl, watching my reflected mouth, my throw up that is greenish and spotted, as I grip the seat.

Mr. Subrahmanian and Megan must see me staring into their

toilet as if it were a wishing well, because Megan says, "Why is she still there?"

"Go fill your sippie with water," Mr. Subrahmanian says and he kneels beside me, stroking my back. "I think our girls must've gotten you sick."

I close the cover down. "I'll clean this all up."

"Please," he says and lifts me to sit on the toilet cover. "This is the least we can do for your staying."

Megan rushes up, cup spilling water, and holds it to my lips. I gulp in one long swig and Mr. Subrahmanian, jingling out keys from his pockets, says, "Let me take you home."

I push myself up—wobbling—but chop-step Ramu-style to the door, then the stairs. "I can bike back."

It will be the last time I see that house, as I straddle my bike and pull slowly away. On the ride down the asphalt road, one of many leading from houses with rose gardens to the campus with cops, I will turn out the complex and veer too sharply into corner shrubs. I will fall off and, for several minutes, will lie on the pavement, cars whizzing by, beside an elm like the one that had buckled that other concrete where I'd waited for Ma and Deeta to call me. They'd stood like tiny sentinels behind the screen, eyes lurid saucers, and while Deeta stood with an unsure palm on the handle, Ma had popped her neck and said, "Don't think you can come back!" I will remember the light grayer than it is here, falling on buildings crumbling with kids running between them, and I will murmur the epitaph scattered like puff on my train ride out: *Dios te bendiga.*

Though the only thing that feels blessed, three years out of the Bronx, one sick day out of the gated mansion, is that I'm sitting beside Kosal in the Veteran's Hall, no matter how momentarily. He's wearing a white silk kurta I bought him, paper cups of chaat and chai steaming before us, though for now we clench each other's hands and watch the Yolo desis come and go.

"Isn't that your boss?" he says, pointing to Mrs. Subrahmanian in a black-and-gold sari with white tea roses braided through her bun. She's showing off Nena, dressed in a ghagra, ribbons in her hair, to a few other IT types, also mothers who drag their doll-like children behind them.

"God," I say. "I hope she doesn't see me."

"If you hate it there so much, why don't you leave?"

"It's the only thing I've got till I start the teaching job."

"You underestimate yourself, Mali."

After dinner, the young desis, mostly science grad students newly arrived from the South Indian cities, dance in a frantic crowd before the deejay. He reminds me of the NYC desi crowd, a hunched-over, cap-and-kicks-wearing Chinese American, cryptically swishing that vinyl, bopping his head to some separate beat. I pull Kosal with me—he grins and snaps his fingers, moving his muscled legs in some funky jiggle all his own—and we dance at the edge of the circle.

But the circle won't open and drifts away: Kosal and I the loosest bodies in the room everyone is watching, the mass of Indian scientists who will not acknowledge us. A silk-scarfed uncle who's got an organizer breastpin runs up to the crowd, elbowing through the sweaty backs. "What are you doing? You have to dance with everyone!" Kosal and I smile at each other—it's too late for the circles to merge—and I want to warm my hands over his face, my father's face, a gift that feels like home.

It's then that Megan runs past, yanking apart our hands, but when I reach over to ruffle her hair, she doesn't glance back, darting instead to the other circle. Kosal, who must see the tremor on my face, pulls me in. "She's just a kid."

"I can't do this anymore."

"You don't have to be anything you don't want to be."

Which sounds like a Bihu motto, when everyone—tribal or non-tribal, Hindu or Muslim, even a stray like me—could supposedly gather. Every April, Ma and Deeta would pack us in the Camry,

Ma's Ponds fragrancing the car, Deeta reciting husori lines in his bow-tied suit, a duffel bag of dancing bells between me and Henna. We'd drive two hours to Edison, New Jersey, where Henna and I tumbled into a Presbyterian Hall of light, aluminum trays and Corning dishes laid out on a foldout table, chairs set up for games that were anything but. Henna and I were competitive though not with each other—something I refrain from telling outsiders, who name our distance thus—the will to win some janky toy, to shove some kid's butt off a chair deflated once Henna, always unsure, was trapped in empty space. Her kneading hands only made me want to knock off the punk who'd kicked her from the circle, while she cheered me on, "Mali sit-sit-sit!"

And just like that, I know what to say. Kosal is waiting at the exit as I search for my gray pea coat in the hall coat rack, and Mrs. Subrahmanian comes up, her first hello all evening. Mr. Subrahmanian reins in the girls to his sides and Mrs. Subrahmanian says, "Did you enjoy yourself? I didn't know you celebrated Diwali."

"Why wouldn't I?" I say, toggling up my coat. "By the way, I'm not coming back."

She looks at Kosal, who nods slowly at me. "My parents arrive next week. How will I manage till December?"

"You know what my mother said when I said I was working for you? She said even she wouldn't hire me"

Mrs. Subrahmanian flinches. "Everyone has different criteria."

"My mother didn't have a real choice but I do. You make me think I'm lucky she was around."

Mrs. Subrahmanian steps closer, that blue blood rushing life at last to her uptilted face. "You are like our daughters, Nirmali. I'll double your wages."

And just like that, I turn away, clasping Kosal's hand through the files exiting the double doors, walking gingerly along lampless streets to the purple hippie house. Until on a side street with a flickering electric candle, Kosal hauls me up on his back and my feet, throbbing in white kitten heels, swing up cool as air.

SNOW LIONS

Though the office gig won't start till December—a whole month more of hand-to-mouth—I'm itching to leave the guys too. Which may be how, one week into biking Davis blocks strewn with figs and cherries and apples rotting beside fences, counting whether I should sell my records, my eggs, or the bike beneath me, I show up at Delhi Delight. It's right before a Friday dinner shift I haven't been given and, as I bustle past the men plating tables, I wonder if Ramu's mentioned the job drama to Gerald.

Gerald's slouched at the bar, sipping beer-foaming shots and thumbing through the menus, presumably for a million more fusion items to add. He fidgets when I stand glaring before him, as if no one's supposed to see him hiding between the back row of flasks, the sample bottles beside him.

"What's going on with my days?" I say. "Why am I getting one call a week when you told me you needed four nights? I could've looked for other work!"

Gerald throws up his hands. "My wife makes the schedule." He sidles out the bar gate and steps behind the buffet trays, pretending to look for napkins. "Why does everyone think I can solve all their problems?"

I stride over and slap my palms on the table corner—trays rattle—Gerald jumps—the chefs and dishwashers crowd the dining hall entrance, eager spectators. "Am I supposed to pay my rent on your jokes, Gerald? Give me notice if you don't want me 'cause I need steady work."

"Calm down," he says, slipping out his Nokia, dialing hurriedly. The men glance at each other half- knowingly, as Gerald *mmhmm*s and *but*s to his wife's high, relentless tone. He hangs up and frowns at me. "She says there aren't enough days for everyone. And that you are rude to her and forgetful with the customers."

"When," I say. "Give me examples."

Gerald adjusts his tie and says, "How should I know? Only you two know and I'm getting caught in the middle." He smiles slightly, as if being a middleman were like winning a fucking prize.

Ramu rests a hand on Gerald's shoulder. "Boss, Mali is good girl. There must be some misunderstanding."

"Forget it," I say, crumpling my black tie, tossing it into the nearest tray. "I want my pay for the whole last month."

Gerald frowns at the tie-ball, as if he doesn't understand why it's not aloo gobi. "Ramu is right. This is all a misunderstanding. Though hours don't grow on trees you know. Still. I'll see if I can find some for you."

I'm already writing down my address on a yellow stickie, which I give to Ramu. "He can mail me here. Good luck. I hope you all stay in business."

Ramu runs after me as I jet for the front door. "Come by the house again. I give you paycheck and surprise."

I'm shaking my head but Ramu, ever the hustler, has already turned to the kitchen. "I'll fix things quick-quick, Mali. You'll see."

Not quick enough: Kosal's visiting his folks in Long Beach till Thanksgiving, Ma won't talk to me long enough to make the holiday home, and Henna, a financier who wouldn't know if I did have cancer, probably wouldn't pick up my call even then. I marathon-ring the Woodland school district instead and begin waking at 6:00 for 8:00 a.m. subbing gigs, one day gathering toys tornadoed by five year olds until lunchtime liberation, another day chalking up grammar to mouthy fifth graders till one of us caves from boredom. When I do show up on Ramu's stoop, two weekends out from Diwali hope, it's Tashi who cracks open the door and reaches out her good hand again: an envelope this time that, according to her block letters, holds my CHECK and TICKET. "Our gift. Don't lose it, huh? One of us will take you there."

A promise that tides me, with four miracle days of high school music and Deeta's insistent, mailed check, till the next weekend. I'm wearing a seersucker dress Kosal selected and gripping Tashi's slight envelope as she drives us single-handed to a school, atop one of these endless San Francisco hills. Kids are gathered in the small playground, squirming and singing, their mismatched words tinkling down to the Corolla, under a strangely cloudless sky. The teacher pauses and they try again, a low chant punctuated by an off-key flute, and I'm almost back in the Shillong hills with its Catholic churches, its Khasi ladies with their elegantly done toenails, its nearly inaudible hum of tribal tunes and war dirges. "Shillong-Shillong-Shillong," Ma would joke, as she does out of earshot, back from some insufferable party. "Anytime anyone sees anything pretty, they say it's like Shillong. Call it like it is!"

Tashi thinks I'm laughing at the kids and waves out at them. "They can't say it right, huh? But you must have been like this too." She steers the car slowly around to the Berkeley Marina, where Tibetans in heavy beads and embroidered skirts are streaming into an oblong pier-side hotel. "Enjoy it," she pats my lap. "Ramu and I will pick you up at three."

The Tibetan Association of the Bay Area has rented out the penthouse, so that whenever you turn across the single circle wall of window, you look down at the Pacific, unbelievably blue and still. I feel breathless, as if I might keel right through glass into sea, so I sink down along a back-section of window, under a dance-like rail, and settle cross-legged on the carpet, yoga-breathing.

Several minutes later, a round-faced woman with a blue striped scarf bends over me. Her peppery hair is surprisingly curly, like mine, so that she has the look of a grizzled lioness.

"South Indian?" she says, scarf-mopping her face. She squints at my nametag. "Nir-mali Raj-bon . . ."

I flinch. Duskier than anyone else in my family, the only one with double lids and a thinnish nose, I'm used to this or Bengali. "Assamese. Tibetan?"

The speaker is asking us to find our tables and the room swirls with bodies rushing past the wall-high windows, the crystal-laden tables and I am herded to the backmost corner, seated next to skeptical Lion Lady. She ignores me through the samosa and momo appetizers, closing her eyes to listen to the opening act, a Tibetan classical singer. I keep my back to the stage, chewing the chicken filling and trying to hold his high, crystalline voice. But when the refrain blossoms into a careening-off-course woman's keening, I turn. An exquisite young guy with long, loose hair, elegant bones and hound eyes stalks about the stage, enacting a story I can't make out exactly, carving away at a small violin-or-guitar-like-thing.

Skeptical Lion Lady taps me. "How you like?"

"I wish I knew what he was saying."

She nods sagely—"snow lions"—and closes her eyes again.

Though this is not the creature or place she or he means, I'm back in the Bronx, knee-deep in snow. I've got a shovel in my hands, which I can barely feel like my lump, but like my lump, I know is there. I know I've got to make something of this. I've got to dig us out. And I'm digging around our car, Ma on the other side, both of us bundled like Inuits in black bubble coats, in black Timberlands, in scarves that Ma must have knitted the days she was home but that are soaked through. And the snow is spearing slanted at us so hard, that these hours of scooping up the snow seems futile, and I want to cry over to Ma, who is rubbing her shoulders (they are coming out her sockets), *go home, go inside, go where it's warm.* Deeta and Henna are inside the house of course, just a couple yards away, but minutes and hours in this snow and they don't ever peek out the window. Instead the snow carries off my unsaid words too. The snow thumps down in lumps now, so that the largest, iciest hail I've ever seen barrage us, like celestial bullets, and still, we cannot stop our work. We cannot escape the cold. We must dig out the car, else how will we ever move? So I drop the shovel and lift my face, my wet gloves to the hail, and the throbbing warms up my blue-sore body, gives a crescendo to the heart behind my knee that stabs and dips like the last notes of an outlawed opera.

It is the school kids, who'd sung upon the San Francisco hilltops, who follow the Tibetan man and his snow lions. All through their skits, their dances, the emcee interrupts to define again and again the word *thanks*. She is a sprightly lady with pixie hair who talks about generosity, about occupation, about welcome. As she talks, on and on to this room of mostly Tibetans, some Americans, white and black, and a handful of Indians, I wonder what Tashi is trying to say. She talks about how the happy man is the grateful man, how to be wealthy is to give away in this room of very moneyed folks— and Tibetans are turning to their dinner guests, draping white silk scarves around their necks. I sit for a cold moment, guessing I will be passed over, but Skeptical Lion Lady faces me. "Thank you," she says, bowing without smiling, stroking each line of the scarf down my ribs, my knees. "Thank you for your friendship in this place."

Biographical Note

Reema Rajbanshi is a creative and critical writer born in Miami and raised in the Bronx. Her short stories have been published in print and online journals such as *Chicago Quarterly Review* and *Blackbird* and explore the nonlinear lines of girlhood, violence, and migration. As a graduate of the UC Davis writing program, she plays with semi-experimental forms and crafts narratives of the body. As a graduate of UC San Diego in literature, her research work on global indigeneities, Brazil, and Northeast India also appear across her creative fiction and nonfiction. Among her awards and fellowships are travel grants from her alma mater, Harvard University, and a Pushcart Prize nomination. She currently teaches at Haverford College and lives in Philadelphia, Pennsylvania. *Sugar, Smoke, Song* is her first book.